HARA-KIRI

BY CRAIG DILOUIE

HARA-KIRI

A NOVEL OF THE PACIFIC WAR

CRAIG DILOUIE

HARA-KIRI
A novel of the Pacific War
©2018 Craig DiLouie. All rights reserved.

Editing by Timothy Johnson.
Cover art by Eloise Knapp Design.
Book layout by Ella Beaumont.

Published by ZING Communications, Inc.

www.CraigDiLouie.com

Area of operation. The Philippines.

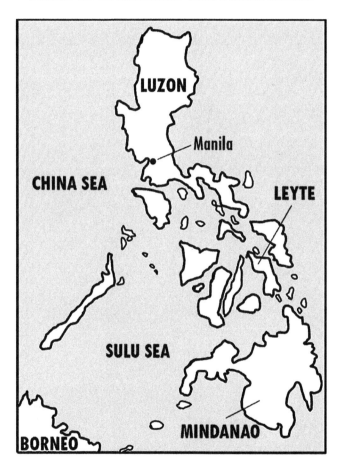

CHAPTER ONE

CHANGING OF THE GUARD

Captain Howard Saunders called all hands to quarters.

The crew mustered under the hot sun on the *Sandtiger*'s salt-stained deck. Lt. Grady, Lt. Percy, and Lt. Nixon stood in dress whites, while the sailors arrayed in neat rows behind them in their white hats and dungarees.

And Lt. Commander Charlie Harrison, USN, sweated in his high-necked white tunic while his heart pounded against the decorations lining his chest. Never in combat had he felt as nervous as he did now.

He filled his lungs with air and bawled, "Attennnnnnnshun!"

Vice Admiral Charles Lockwood, Captain Squadron Commander Rich Cooper, and their entourage crossed the gangplank while the Navy band played "Semper Paratus" on the pier.

All hands saluted in unison. The senior officers

returned it. As the band finished, Vice Admiral Lockwood paraded, inspecting the men.

He paused before Charlie. "You believe in destiny, Harrison?"

"I believe in its pursuit, sir."

The man smiled. "Let's just say I thought we'd be doing this one day."

"Thank you for your faith, sir."

The admiral pinned the Navy Cross to Charlie's tunic. "Congratulations on an outstanding war patrol. You seem to enjoy taking the fight to the enemy on land, but we're hoping this new posting will keep you in the Navy a while."

Charlie smiled back. "Thank you, sir."

Lockwood inspected the crew next, pausing to pin the Silver Star to Machinist's Mate John Braddock's chest. The big sailor's sour expression broke into an incredulous grin. They shook hands.

Satisfied with his inspection, Lockwood returned to Cooper's side. One of the admiral's aides read aloud a letter of commendation for the patrol to Saipan, noting Chief McDonough's posthumous award of the Navy Cross. Every man would have a copy placed in his service record. Many had received their dolphins, and all were authorized to wear the Submarine Combat Pin with three stars, recognizing the *Sandtiger*'s four consecutive war patrols with one or more ships sunk.

This done, Charlie commanded the men to parade rest. Under his feet, one of the deadliest war machines ever built lay moored to the pier. A *Gato*-class submarine displacing 1,500 tons of water, the *Sandtiger* was over 300 feet long and twenty-seven feet wide at the beam. Six forward tubes, four aft, fitted with a complement of twenty-four torpedoes. Her four diesel engines drove her at a top speed of twenty knots on the surface, while her four electric motors allowed a top submerged speed of nine knots. She could dive to 300 feet and range 11,000 miles.

The Navy Yard at Mare Island had refurbished her inside and out, including a fresh coat of black and gray paint, a five-inch deck gun, upgraded SJ radar, and a streamlined superstructure that allowed her to sail with a minimized silhouette.

The *Sandtiger* still had her scars, visible even with the new paint job. The Imperial Japanese Navy had mauled her more than once. Still, she'd delivered far worse than she'd gotten and survived every encounter. Her proud battle flag waved on the clothesline stretching from the bow to the periscope supports, displaying a grinning shark in a sailor's hat along with numerous patches bragging of ships sunk. Seventeen sinkings in five patrols, nearly 50,000 tons, while logging enough miles to circle the globe twice.

She still had many more miles to go and many more fights before this war ended.

"We are winning this war," Admiral Lockwood told the crew. "But we haven't won it yet. With so much at stake, the Navy must have the right men commanding the submarines. It's a job for tough, decisive leaders. You men were lucky to have such a man in your commanding officer, Captain Howard Saunders."

Lockwood pinned the Silver Star to Saunders's tunic and shook his hand. "Read your orders of detachment, Captain."

Captain Saunders read his orders aloud and finished: "Haul down my flag."

Crewmen lowered the captain's pennant while the band flourished, ending with the crash of a gun salute. While the awards ceremony was highly formalized, the ritual of changing command was even more formal and steeped in Navy tradition. The ceremony officially transferred responsibility and authority over a U.S. warship from one commanding officer to another. All hands mustered had a clear view of the proceedings, as it required the entire crew to bear witness.

Saunders said, "I am ready to be relieved."

Captain Squadron Commander Cooper handed Charlie an envelope. "Read your orders, if you please, Mr. Harrison."

Charlie opened it and found two carefully folded sheets of paper.

He unfolded the first. It showed a Varga girl lying naked on pillows, giving him a mischievous look over her bare shoulder.

Charlie shot a glance at Rusty and Percy, who smirked while keeping their eyes fixed straight ahead.

He cleared his throat and unfolded the second sheet. "To Lt. Commander Charles Frederick Harrison, USN. Report no later than September 8, 1944 to USS *Sandtiger* at Pearl Harbor Submarine Base. Upon arrival on board, report to Howard Saunders, commanding officer, USS *Sandtiger* for duty as his relief. Then report to the immediate superior in command. Signed, Vice Admiral Charles Lockwood, Commander, Submarine Force, U.S. Pacific Fleet."

His mouth gone dry, Charlie swallowed hard and saluted Saunders. "I relieve you, sir."

Saunders returned the salute. "I stand relieved."

"Break my flag," Charlie commanded.

Crewmen raised his pennant to full honors.

"Scared?" Saunders murmured to him as the band played.

"Yes," Charlie said.

"The boat's in good hands. Do your duty and never look back. You'll do fine."

"Thank you, Captain."

"You're the captain now."

After the ritual ended with firing guns, Charlie marched forward to salute Cooper. "Sir, I have properly relieved Howard Saunders as commanding officer of the *Sandtiger* and report to duty."

Cooper returned the salute. "Very well, Captain."

Charlie turned to address the crew, the faces of the young men who'd survived the Sea of Japan with him, who'd sailed with him to Saipan. "The sand tiger is a very cunning shark, a night feeder that hunts by stealth. The Electric Boat Company built our *Sandtiger* well. She has fought hard and taken good care of us. But you are her fighting spirit. Submarining is a team effort, and I couldn't ask for a better crew. I'm proud to take command and continue *Sandtiger*'s winning streak begun by Captain Moreau and continued by Captain Saunders, whom we all wish well. As far as what comes next, I'll simply quote Captain Mush Morton: 'Stay on the bastard until he's on the bottom.' We keep doing that, we can all go home."

The crew broke protocol by erupting into a full-throated cheer.

Charlie said into the din, "All standing orders and regulations remain in effect. Mr. Grady, you may take charge and dismiss the ship's company."

The band struck up a plucky rendering of "Bravura" as the crew cheered again and swarmed below deck to the reception held in the wardroom and crew's mess.

Rusty grinned. "You ready for this?"

Charlie smiled but said nothing.

His friend changed his question to a statement of fact. "You're ready for this."

"Yes," Charlie said, surprised by a surge of confidence. "I'm ready."

"Remember what I told you. Half the job is doing, the other half is acting like you know what you're doing."

"I'll remember. Nice touch with the Varga girl, by the way."

Rusty laughed. "Another reminder for you. You got to hang loose to make it in the submarines."

"Duly noted. Again."

"That and to show you what we're all fighting for, brother."

During the invasion of Saipan, American bombers flew their first raid since the Doolittle raid of 1942. Nearly fifty B-29s based in India bombed the steel works at Yawata. The following month, American Marines completed the conquest of Saipan and liberated Guam. By August, they captured all the Marianas.

Now the Pearl Harbor Naval Base buzzed with news American forces had invaded Morotai and Peleliu. Soon, bombers would be able to stage from the Marianas and pound Tokyo on a daily basis. American grunts would continue battling their way straight to Honshu. The scuttlebutt was Taiwan or the Philippines were the next target for invasion. Taking either one would cut the Japanese home islands from their supply of oil, rubber, bauxite, coal, foodstuffs, cloth, and other materials that fed their insatiable war machine.

Meanwhile, the submarines would go on doing their part to starve the beast and shorten the war. Charlie chafed at the idea of attending the reception even though it was in his honor. He was captain now, the object of his hopes and destiny. What he wanted was orders. A fresh patrol in good hunting grounds.

He couldn't wait to get back into the fight and see it through to the end. He couldn't wait to see what else his destiny had in store for him.

CHAPTER TWO

NO PEDESTAL

In the red gloom of the Officer's Club, Charlie sipped his scotch alone at a corner booth. He smiled at the busy waitresses plowing through cigarette smoke drifts with their trays of drinks. He thought of Evie, who wrote him a letter every week. And Jane, who didn't, but still frequented his thoughts.

Things were looking up for him.

The *Sandtiger* had completed her voyage and combat repairs, along with a few upgrades. Per Navy policy, a quarter of the crew had rotated to new construction, but aside from the chief machinist's mate—and Smokey, the chief quartermaster—he hadn't lost any important personnel. Rusty had agreed to stay on as exec, which the Navy approved along with other staffing requests.

As well it should! The Navy owed him. In a heavy fog on the Celebes Sea, he'd sunk an aircraft carrier. He'd hammered his way out of the

Sea of Japan and destroyed the Meteor, the giant coastal defense gun, on Saipan. Before earning his present rank, the Navy awarded him two Silver Stars, two Navy Crosses, and two Purple Hearts.

Normally a moderate drinker, Charlie found himself drunk. The scotch erased his usual self-doubt and buoyed his ego. Gone was the fatigue that had plagued him before Saipan. His impending confrontation with cleithrophobia didn't bother him. He'd done it. He'd made captain, and now all he wanted was the chance to get back out there and sink Japanese ships.

In a week, he'd sail back into the war, and he expected the squadron commander to give him choice hunting grounds. Something big was about to happen, he could feel it. Whatever it was, he was certain the *Sandtiger* would play a part, with him leading her into combat.

This afternoon, he'd taken a break from the attack trainer to seek out other captains for advice. Dick O'Kane of the *Tang*, who'd apprenticed under Mush Morton; Eugene "Lucky" Fluckey of the *Barb*, who'd revolutionized night surface attacks by joining a convoy from astern before shooting; and Sam "The Destroyer Killer" Dealey of the *Harder*. The men had gone, but the effects of multiple glasses of scotch lingered. This last one was purely for celebration, the first time

Charlie truly basked in his moment. After this, he'd splurge on a nice, juicy steak and maybe catch a movie.

For the first time in months, tonight was just for Charlie Harrison.

Rusty found him grinning into his glass.

"Good for you!" he said.

"Hey." Charlie stiffened his posture into some semblance of an officer and a gentleman. "What's good for me?"

"Hanging loose. Making it. Submarines. You can't spend all your time in the attack trainer. Percy goes a bit overboard with his good times, but you could learn from him."

"I'm doing a different kind of learning today."

Rusty sat and waved his hand for service. "Care to explain that?"

Charlie told him he'd spoken with other captains to learn the lessons no school or trainer could teach him. He'd bought them all drinks and listened to their tales, gleaning wisdom from their triumphs and mistakes.

"Great idea," Rusty said. "They must have some amazing stories. I'm sorry I missed it. Where'd they go?"

"They cleared out."

Strange, how it happened. O'Kane, Fluckey, and Dealey had all heard of Charlie but appeared uncertain what to make of what they'd heard. They'd been friendly enough but excused themselves the first chance they had, as if he were a torpedo running hot in the tube.

"I don't know," he said. "Maybe I intimidated them a little. The whole *Hara-kiri* thing. All the stories going around."

Rusty chuckled. "Brother, you are wasted. You want the truth?"

"Of course I want the truth."

"Rig for collision, buddy."

"Just spit it out already."

He trusted his friend's judgment. From the bombing of Cavite to Saipan, Rusty had seen a lot of the fighting. He'd grown wise about war and Navy culture.

"They think you're bad luck," Rusty told him.

Charlie started. "What did *I* do?"

"I don't know, let's see. Every patrol you've been on, the captain either got killed, sick, or lost his nerve. The Navy may be a lot of things, but one thing's for sure, it's superstitious."

"But I..." Charlie stopped. There was nothing to say. Superstition wasn't something you could reason with.

In the old days of wooden sailing ships, sailors threw coins into the foam and poured wine on the deck. They wore tattoos to ward off evil spirits. After getting their crew cuts, they wouldn't trim their hair or nails again until the voyage was over. They spat into the harbor before launching.

Today, the Navy had fewer pervasive rituals, though plenty developed around each particular ship. When Charlie served on the *Kennedy*, the captain forbade the washing of coffee mugs until the end of the voyage. On the *Sabertooth*, the sailors threw coins to the crowd on the pier for safekeeping. On the *Sandtiger*, Percy used to wear his Aloha shirts. When the submarine originally launched, a bottle of champagne was broken against her bow, harkening back to the days of Vikings and Greeks greasing the skids with blood, which became wine and eventually the more celebratory champagne.

A waitress delivered Rusty's drink. He sipped it and laughed. "I'm surprised Cooper let you on another boat, much less make captain."

His friend was onto something, as usual. The realization sobered him. "You just knocked me right off my pedestal. I guess I had it coming."

"Brother, this is the Navy. There ain't any pedestal."

"Well, you agreed to stay on as my exec. I take it you're not the superstitious type."

"Actually, I am. And you're my lucky charm."

Certain now Rusty was messing with him, Charlie threw him a dark look. "How am I your lucky charm, exactly?"

"Every time you're on a boat, it goes through hell but makes it out okay, for starters. Plus you're a new captain, at the bottom of the totem pole, and that means two things you can take to the bank. One, Cooper only gives busy shipping lanes to senior captains, so we're in for a nice, quiet patrol. Two, there's a torpedo shortage. We'll be lucky if we get even half our usual number of fish. Can't do a lot of fighting if we don't have torpedoes in the tubes. I wanted to see the end of the war, not die in it. Lucy and Rusty Junior are counting on me coming home."

"I thought..." Charlie let out a bitter laugh at his inflated sense of self-importance. "I had this idea... There's no pedestal, is there?"

Rusty sipped his scotch and sighed. "No, there is not."

Charlie tasted bile and stood. "Hold that thought."

With that, he staggered off to the head and emptied his guts.

He told himself he'd never drink too much again, especially on an empty stomach, especially when there was any chance of getting sucker-punched.

He'd fought hard, did some amazing things in the war, and earned the rank of captain. But that didn't buy him any special favors. The Navy

14

didn't give a crap about him. He was starting all over, a simple fact.

The best lessons always hurt.

When he returned to the table far more sober and humble than he left it, Rusty raised his glass. "Welcome to command, Charlie."

CHAPTER THREE

NEW BLOOD

From a pier at the Submarine Base, Charlie watched the *Sandtiger* steam across the harbor after her shakedown cruise. Once a destroyer officer, he'd considered submarines big, ugly sewer pipes, but now he admired her sleek superstructure. Her low profile and gray paint ensured virtual invisibility at night. Her modest size belied her ability to stalk and take down much larger prey. She was a hunter, a little shark with a giant bite, and she was his.

Evie had accused him of marrying the war and giving his heart to it when he should keep himself tethered to home. Charlie wasn't sure she was right about that anymore, but knew he felt something like love for this boat. At sea, the *Sandtiger* delivered unparalleled freedom, power, purpose—the opportunity to test and prove himself. In a short time, he and the boat would fuse into a single predatory organism.

Manned by Relief Crew 202 of the AS-19 *Proteus*, which lay moored nearby, the *Sandtiger* blasted its whistle and warped alongside the pier. Captain Harvey bawled orders on the bridge.

"All stop! Cast the mooring lines!"

The able fifteen-man crew quickly secured the submarine to the pier.

The refit and relief crews played an important role in the war effort. They helped repair submarines returned to port while the combat crews enjoyed a few weeks of liberty. They cleaned the insides and scraped barnacles, which reduced fuel efficiency and speed, from the hull. And they gave the boats a thorough fitness test before returning them to sea.

Charlie was eager to know how the *Sandtiger* had fared in her shakedown. Before Saipan, he'd gone out with her, and manned by this very relief crew, the ship had nosedived nearly to the bottom. A piece of a Japanese destroyer had gummed up her works.

As sailors threw down the gangplank, however, he stayed put. Captain Harvey had no love for him, and today, he was in command, the master of the *Sandtiger*.

Wearing a .45 on his hip, the deck watch crossed the gangplank and took his post.

"How'd she sail today?" Charlie said.

The man smiled in the hot September sun.

"Tip top, sir. She's seaworthy." His accent was pure Brooklyn.

"How did the countermeasures do?"

The *Sandtiger* had received a brand new upgrade during her refitting. Special countermeasures that would help the submarine escape enemy ships during a depth charging. Only a handful of boats in the entire Pacific had them.

Amazing technology. He hoped it worked.

"Can't help you there," the sailor said. "We were told to leave those alone. Hey, you're that guy, aren't you? *Hara-kiri*. You are, right?"

Charlie usually found the nickname startling and even embarrassing when said aloud, but today, it made him glower in a simmering rage.

"I'm Lt. Commander Harrison."

"I remember you from that day we took a nosedive in this boat," the sailor said happily. "That was a day."

Captain Harvey noticed Charlie standing on the pier. Thinking Charlie's scowl was for him, he scowled back. Apparently, he also considered Charlie bad luck, the reason he was still stuck in a relief crew instead of getting his own boat. Charlie was glad he'd stayed on the pier. He'd learned some humility yesterday, but he wasn't about to take orders or abuse on his own boat.

Another officer emerged from the bridge hatch. Morrison was slim and tall, too tall for a submarine, red-faced and sweating after the morning's angles and dangles.

"What's your name, sailor?" Charlie said.

"Signalman Third Class Bernard Schwartz, sir."

"Mr. Schwartz, kindly pass a message to Mr. Morrison I'd like a word."

"The exec, huh? Sure."

Like all relief crews across the Pacific, Relief Crew 202 comprised recent graduates from Submarine School. While some graduates lucked out with a plum assignment to new construction—becoming one of the "plank crew" on a new boat—many served on relief crews before assignment. Morrison hadn't been able to transfer to active duty aboard a submarine. It wasn't hard to guess why. Harvey was punishing him for taking the conn during the nosedive.

Charlie needed a new officer.

Morrison stomped across the gangplank. "You blew up the Meteor!"

Charlie growled, "A team blew up the Meteor, one of whom is dead."

He'd seen the young officer in action. The man could think in a crisis. No further testing needed. Charlie wanted him on his crew.

But he wasn't having any hero-worship stuff.

Whatever his accomplishments, their retelling made them sound far more incredible than he remembered them. For him, the assault on the giant coastal gun had been a blur, revisited in slow, painful detail only in his nightmares.

To his credit, Morrison took the hint and stiffened his posture. "Well done, anyway. What can I do for you, Commander?"

Charlie handed over an envelope. "You can come work for me, Lieutenant, and earn your own stories."

The officer tore it open and scanned his orders, his lips moving as he read. "You're kidding me. Is this for real?"

"You're done with the *Proteus*. I'm hoping you can handle a deck gun crew."

"It's only my favorite part of the boat! We fire a few rounds every time we take a boat out for a test run. I bring a few barrels, and we practice on them."

"With the torpedo shortage, we're getting stiffed on fish."

Cooper had given him the bad news this morning. The *Sandtiger* would go out with less than half her usual complement of torpedoes. Enough to fill the tubes but nothing to reload.

Morrison grinned as he got it. "So we might see some gun work."

"We'll be bringing extra ammunition for the deck gun," Charlie told him. "As a junior captain,

I can't promise a lot of action on the next patrol. I doubt we'll get a good patrol area. But we'll look for trouble wherever we can find it."

His next patrol wouldn't be like the last two to Saipan and the Sea of Japan. The Navy was planning some big operation. He sensed it, but as a novice captain, he didn't qualify for any special missions. After the *Sandtiger* refueled at Midway, he'd receive his sealed patrol orders and find out what ComSubPac wanted him to do and where. He had no illusions, following his sobering talk with Rusty, that they'd give him a busy shipping lane.

Still, as he'd said, that wouldn't prevent him from seeking any opportunity.

Morrison squinted into the distance. "Boarding party. That'd do just fine."

"Excuse me?"

"What we'll need is a boarding party. A gang of volunteers. Men ready to support the gun crew with small arms. Commandos. We'll make gasoline bombs."

Charlie smiled. He'd obviously found the right man for the job. "Come up with a plan. We sail in less than a week."

The lieutenant's face lit up again. "The plan is we're going to kill Japs."

Charlie saw his own eagerness and ambition reflected in Morrison's face, coupled with

Moreau's frank bloodlust. The *Sandtiger* was mean, she fought dirty, and she was a street fighter. Morrison and his commandos would fit right in.

"Welcome to the *Sandtiger*," he said.

They shook hands.

"I thought I was going to miss out on this war," Morrison said.

Captain Harvey called out from the bridge: "Commander!"

"Yes, Captain?"

Grinning like a shark, the captain started to say something but thought better of his choice of words because his crew was listening. "We have important work to do here! I'd appreciate it if you didn't pester my crew and waste their time!"

Charlie called back, "You mean *my* crew, Captain!"

The little things. They really did get you through a war.

"See you soon, Lieutenant," he said and shoved off.

Behind him, he heard the relief crew cheer as Morrison shared his good news.

Next stop, the Royal Hawaiian, where he'd find John Braddock.

CHAPTER FOUR

HAIL TO THE CHIEF

A half hour later, Charlie approached the Royal Hawaiian Hotel with its Moorish architecture and concrete stucco walls painted a trendy coral pink. Once a luxury hotel catering to the well-to-do, the Pink Palace of the Pacific now exclusively served Navy personnel on R&R.

He found Machinist's Mate John Braddock sprawled on a lounge chair at the swimming pool, nursing a pink drink with an umbrella sticking out of it. The chair sagged under the weight of the gorilla-sized sailor.

"It's no use," Charlie said. "You're still white as a fish. You're probably giving the sun a sunburn."

The machinist shaded his eyes against the bright tropical sun and glared. "Here comes trouble. The answer is 'no' to whatever you're selling."

"You might want to hear what I'm selling before saying anything."

Braddock stood and held out his drink. "Hang on to this for me for a minute."

This done, the man stomped off toward the beach.

Charlie watched him go. Then it hit him. Braddock was ditching him. He shook his head and set off in pursuit.

Servicemen in bathing suits crowded the sands, sunbathing and playing volleyball and otherwise showing off for a few smiling Hawaiian girls. Concertina wire barriers separated the beachfront from neighboring civilian beaches. Braddock could try to swim for it, but otherwise Charlie had him cornered.

The sailor glanced over his shoulder and growled, "You still here? You already had your chance to kill me!"

"Can you hold up and hear me out?"

"Quit following me!"

With his fists clenched, Braddock marched toward the hotel garden, which was rich with coconut trees and bright red ginger blossoms.

Charlie sighed. "I'm not going to chase you all over this hotel."

"I'm going back to my relief crew after liberty!"

He held up some papers. "See, that's the thing..."

The sailor stopped and sagged. "God damn Navy. Promises don't mean anything."

"I'm—"

Braddock wheeled. "The Japs are using suicide torpedoes now! You know about the *kaiten*? They're Type 93s with a suicide pilot. He sails it right into your hull. Maniacs are fighting the war now."

"I've—"

"No wonder you made captain. I could see you piloting a *kaiten* yourself."

"For crying out loud, Braddock—"

"Why?" the man pleaded. "Tell me that at least. You really want to get me killed, is that it? Or is it just revenge for some stupid jokes I pulled to pass the time? You want me doing shit work in your engine rooms, is that it?"

"Well, that's what the chief machinist does," Charlie said. "So yes."

"That's what I—what did you say?"

"When you return to the *Sandtiger*, you'll head the engine department."

The sailor glared even more ferociously at him. "Why?"

"Because I can count on you," Charlie told him. "If you're saying I take risks, you're right. Those risks can pay off big, but they also make messes. You're good at fixing messes. And I need chiefs like Smokey. Men who will tell me how they see it and make sure the crew doesn't get hurt by my messes."

27

His compliments only further enraged the sailor, and Charlie had to struggle not to smile.

"You got the wrong guy," Braddock fumed.

"You helped me sink the *Mizukaze* at Blanche Bay—"

"That wasn't bravery. That was self-defense."

"And saved the boat when it was out of control when Hunter took on *Yosai*—"

"I stuck a wet toothbrush between two cut power lines, so what?"

"Mindanao, getting *Sabertooth* back on propulsion after we finally sank *Yosai*, Saipan. You may not like hearing it, but you earned your promotion."

"Chief, huh?" A flicker of pleasure crossed his face before he scowled again. "Don't think for a minute I'd be obligated or anything. To be nice to you."

"If you respect the rank, especially in front of the men, you can talk man to man to me anytime. And one other thing. On my boat, shit rolls uphill, not down. You want to bitch, you come to me and do it to my face. I know if you step up—"

"All right," Braddock said. "All right! Stop talking. You got yourself a chief."

"Good. I never thought I'd have to talk a man into a promotion."

"It's just..." The sailor looked away. "Thank you, sir."

For once, saying "sir" like he meant it.

"All right," Charlie said, unsettled. God, the big gorilla had started to choke up, something he never thought he'd see. "Here are your orders."

For all his misanthropy, Braddock didn't want power, and he didn't entirely want to be left alone, either. He wanted somebody to recognize his worth.

Charlie might have appreciated the moment if he believed it signaled a permanent change of character, but Braddock was still Braddock. If Charlie let his guard down, he'd pay for it. He was a risk-taker, though, and that extended to picking his crew.

He wanted the best he could get, period.

"Chief Braddock," the sailor said, trying it on for size. He held out his paw for the drink Charlie still held. "If you don't mind, sir."

Charlie handed it over and watched him take a swig.

Apparently liking the sound of things, Braddock turned and puffed out his hairy chest in response to some imaginary interruption. "What? That's *Chief Petty Officer* Braddock, if you please. That's right. Chief Machinist on the *Sandtiger.*"

"We sail in one—"

Braddock raised his glass. "Hail to the chief!"

Confident he'd made the right decision,

Charlie left the overgrown child to his imaginary conversation.

Submarining was a team sport. If you had the best team, you had the best odds of dealing with any variables and winning the game. Right now, the boat had a wise and capable exec, brilliant engineering officer, talented communications and plotting officer, fire-breathing torpedo and gunnery officer, and a department head who'd keep his engines running no matter what the Japanese threw at it.

A solid crew, and plenty of spare ammo for the deck gun, would make all the difference. He'd squeeze this patrol for every opportunity he could find.

CHAPTER FIVE

FINAL NIGHT

With her repairs complete, the *Sandtiger* was ready to welcome her crew back to the war. Charlie collected his officers in the O-Club and stood them a drink to mark their final night on dry land for the next two and a half months.

Morrison raised his glass. "To killing Japs."

"I can see why you like him," Rusty murmured to Charlie. "He reminds me of somebody."

Percy belted his drink down and waved his hand at the waitress for another round. "You play an instrument, Morrison?"

The young officer shook his head. "I can't even sing in the shower."

"Maybe we'll teach you something. The exec is a grade-A fiddler, and I play the banjo. We taught the captain the harmonica. It worked on him, it should work on you."

"Work on me for what?"

The communications officer snatched Nixon's

beer, downed half of it in a single gulp, and came up for air. "Getting that rudder out of your ass."

"Percy," Charlie warned then turned to Rusty, who was laughing. "Rusty!"

"Definitely reminds me of somebody," his friend said. "Morrison, you're aggressive, and that's good. A guy like you could go far in the submarines. But you—"

"Got to hang loose to make it in the submarines," he and Percy said together.

"Wow," Morrison said. "You really think I could go far?"

"Absolutely." Rusty winked at Charlie.

"I'm planning to stay in after the war ends," the torpedo officer said. "Command my own boat one day. I want to do something, make a difference."

Before Rusty could rib Charlie further, Nixon said, "What about you, Captain? What do you think you'll do after the war?"

"He'll stick with the submarines too," Percy said. "Win the next two wars for us. He's got diesel in his blood, same as Moreau."

Charlie dodged the question. "How about you, Percy?"

"I already gave it some thought. I'm gonna get a backpack and go wherever my feet take me. Keep walking until I sweat this war out of me. See the world without anybody trying to kill me. Go to Tibet, maybe. Learn some wisdom."

The officers nodded, impressed.

"I still have dreams, you know," Percy added. "The bad ones. I'm almost afraid to go home and find out how much I've changed. I'm more afraid I won't make it back at all."

"We're in for a quiet patrol," Rusty said, trying to change the subject. In his view, if you talked about the worst that could happen, it would happen.

Percy waved at the waitress to hurry it up, determined to drink like a fish his last night on dry land. "Yeah, well, watch out. I'm gonna live it up anyway, just in case."

"Peace would be nice," Rusty said.

"Yeah. That goes without saying."

"I mean, I wonder how many people were killed in this war. People who weren't even fighting and wanted nothing to do with it."

"It's why we're fighting," Charlie said. "I know it's a strange thing to say, but we're fighting to save lives. The sooner it's over, the fewer people will have to suffer because of it."

"I don't see that as ironic in the slightest, Skipper," Rusty said. "I'm fighting for my wife and kid. So they stay safe. So I can go home to them. After this is over, I'm done."

Charlie started in surprise. "You'll leave the Navy?"

"I'm going to go to college. I want to learn.

Something I always wanted to do. The funny thing is I would have put it off forever if I hadn't been in combat. Surviving a war makes you think about taking life a little more seriously. Live it in a little more of a hurry."

"What's that Latin saying?" Percy said. "Live for the day."

"Carpe diem," Nixon said.

The communications officer belched. "That's it."

"Peace," Rusty said, as if it were some mythical idea. "I want to live in peace. Just spend time with Lucy and Rusty Junior. Make sure he never has to fight a war like his old man did."

Percy's eye twinkled. "And get busy making more kids."

Rusty smiled with a faraway gaze, as if he could see the future. "I've always wanted a daughter." He returned to the present with a frown. "Though after spending years in the Navy, I'll be terrified when she grows up."

The men hooted with laughter.

Rusty added, "I'll be real thankful to be living in Pittsburgh at that point. No ships or sailors there."

"What do you think you'll study?" Nixon asked him.

"History. So I can figure out why the human race keeps making the same damn mistakes over and over."

Percy picked up the beer in front of Nixon and finished it. Being a teetotaler, the engineering officer didn't mind.

"After the war is over," Nixon said, "I'm going to go into business and get rich."

"You know, I believe you could," Charlie said. The man was scarily smart.

"I only joined the Navy because my father thought it'd be good for me. I learned a lot about engineering. Otherwise, he was dead wrong. I'll invent something and start my own company. Then I'll get to give orders for a change instead of taking them." His eyes darted to Charlie. "No offense, Captain."

"None taken. I think we all know how you feel."

"Shit rolls downhill in the Navy," Rusty agreed. "So what about you, Skipper? You actually gonna stick it out after the war? Get your stars and retire an O-10?"

Charlie had no interest in working his way up to admiral. In fact, he doubted he cared to stay in the Navy at all after this.

"I think I'm with you guys," he said. "At that point, I'll have served my country. I might want to take some years and look after myself."

"And whatever lady you decide on," Percy said with a leer.

"Interesting question, that." Rusty sipped his beer.

"It is," Charlie said, not wanting to talk about Evie and Jane. "But nothing I'm going to think too hard about until I get home."

He did think about it, though.

Evie knew the old Charlie, the ambitious boy who'd joined the Navy to find himself, and she wanted to live a full life with him. Jane knew the new Charlie, the man who'd found himself in war, and she wanted him today because only today was real.

Which of these two wonderful women understood the real Charlie required that Charlie first understand himself. He knew the man he'd been in peace, gotten to know the man he was in war. He didn't know who he'd eventually become when the war was over.

After everything, he had a feeling he'd need to find himself all over again. Despite his feelings for Evie and Jane, he might have to go it alone for a while.

All of which wasn't his crew's business. He might tell Rusty but not the others. It was the captain's prerogative to avoid ribbing and tell his men to mind their business, so he could focus on command.

"The captain walking away from the boats when this is all over," Percy said. "Well, that does it. It really will be peace."

"I'm not sure I believe it," Morrison said, apparently startled at the idea anybody in their right mind would give up command of a fleet submarine.

Percy belched again. "On that note, gents, I'm gonna go find some trouble."

A quick exit, but Charlie had expected nothing less.

"Have fun, but not too much fun," he said. "We need you bright and early."

"Have I ever let you down, Captain?" The communications officer grinned and nudged Nixon. "Come on, let's make tracks while the night's young."

"But I'm enjoying the conversation," Nixon said.

"We'll be smelling these guys' farts for weeks. You can talk then until you're blue in the face. Right now, I need my running buddy."

"Okay, I guess." Nixon's face reddened at the thought of talking to women tonight.

"You make me look good around the ladies." Percy squinted. "What's that word in literature—?"

"Foil," Nixon told him.

"If you say so. Come on, Nix. Time to hit the road."

The engineering officer sighed and rose from his chair. Charlie wondered if leaving the service would be enough to rescue him from taking orders.

Rusty set down his bottle. "I'll be moseying along myself, I think."

Charlie hid his disappointment. "All right."

He'd been all work and no play for weeks, learning the ropes and readying the *Sandtiger* for her next patrol. He'd hoped to really unwind tonight, let it all go just once before returning to the war.

"Talking about Lucy and Rusty," the exec began and stopped to take a breath. "I'm going to write them a letter and turn in."

"I understand." He did. His friend missed them to the point of distraction.

"I'll stay if you want," Morrison said. "We could talk strategy."

Rusty stood and tapped Charlie's shoulder. "See that fella over there? That's Slade Cutter. Just came back from his fourth successful war patrol. The scuttlebutt is he sank five ships, including a submarine."

"Morrison, I think we'll save it for the wardroom," Charlie said, his eyes on Cutter. "Percy's right. We'll have plenty of time."

If he couldn't let go on his last night in port, he'd try to learn something.

Excusing himself, he walked over and introduced himself to the captain of the *Seahorse.*

CHAPTER SIX

PRACTICE MAKES PERFECT

Feeling hot and a little boozy after a few drinks with Slade Cutter, Charlie tossed and turned on his hotel mattress.

Thankfully, the *Seahorse*'s CO hadn't heard of him and had plenty of advice to offer. Hours later, Charlie had left the O-Club feeling even more humbled. While he'd accomplished great things, captains like Cutter were scoring spectacular wins. Pursuing a Japanese convoy for a record eight hours, going head to head with an enemy submarine, sinking three trawlers in the East China Sea with his deck gun.

In 1944, submarining was a whole different ballgame than when Charlie had served under J.R. Kane on the old S-55. In the past few years, the submarine force had learned from its errors, developed new technology and tactics, and gotten very good at killing. Cutter's patrols exemplified what a boat could accomplish with the right leadership and tenacity.

Tomorrow, the *Sandtiger* would sail back into the war, and it'd be Charlie's turn. He'd joined the submarines to find himself and learn what he was really made of by facing death in combat. He'd met that man and liked him. He was about to meet him again, this time under very different circumstances.

While he'd borrowed command, he'd never owned it. Each time he'd taken the conn, the boat had been in crisis, requiring big risks. Leading a patrol from start to finish, he imagined, would be a different thing entirely. He'd have to strike and maintain a perfect balance between caution and audacity, push his men and boat hard without breaking them, and never let his guard down.

These sobering thoughts kept him awake until he jerked out of bed and pulled on his service khakis. He was too wound up for sleep.

He took a walk outside. Because of the blackout rules, the Milky Way sparkled across the clear sky. He had no destination in mind, though he found himself making the long walk to the Submarine Base, ending his trek at the attack trainer.

He chuckled at the feet that had brought him here on their own. Tomorrow, the *Sandtiger* sailed. He'd told himself he was ready for this, but somehow his feet knew he'd never be ready enough.

Well, he thought, *practice makes perfect*. Maybe another night owl, somebody who would help him run a simulation, was awake.

He went in.

And halted in his tracks.

A stunning brunette in an evening dress gaped at him. Her hand flew to her mouth as she let out a little scream.

"It's okay, Barb!" Percy said. "Don't worry, he's on our side."

"Oh." She composed herself and demurely extended her hand. "Hello."

Charlie shook it with a warm smile and said, "What's she doing here?"

"Sinking ships, Cap'n," Percy said.

Looking sheepish, Nixon crept down the stairs, another woman peering from behind him to give Charlie a studied once-over. The women knew they were all in trouble but still eyed him curiously, as he'd often seen them do to submarine captains whose job carried a certain mystique.

Judging from the empty bottles dotting the dummy conning tower, Charlie figured they'd had quite a party. One of Percy's last hurrahs before returning to the war.

"Sorry, Captain," Nixon said. "We didn't mean any harm."

"No harm, no foul, right?" Percy said.

With that, the communications officer offered up his patent insolent smirk, which at times Charlie found endearing and other times made him want to throw a punch. He answered by narrowing his eyes.

"We can go if we aren't allowed to be here," Barb said.

His attention turned to her. "How does she head?"

"Oh-one-seven True," she blurted.

"Battle stations," he said.

"Aye, aye!" the girls shouted.

The attack trainer had been constructed in the same design as the one he'd cut his teeth on back in Submarine School. He and other submarine captains spent many hours here sharpening their skills. Barb stood near the shortened periscope that piped into the room upstairs. Percy happily shambled to the TDC. Nixon and his date hustled up the stairs to operate the circular discs using control cables. These discs moved model ships along a course they'd set up.

"Up scope," Charlie said.

As Charlie pressed the eyepiece for a look up top, he shook his head. Percy's luck with women was a wonder. He chased skirts the way

Moreau had fought the Japanese—fearless, all in, and with nothing to lose. Nixon's luck was even odder considering his chronic shyness, though it didn't hurt that he had a passing resemblance to Cary Grant.

Charlie swept the horizon and spotted the enemy ships crawling across the metal sea with a series of clicks. A freighter, escorted by a destroyer pacing off the port bow. Nixon had set up an easy problem. He'd show the girls how submarining was done by sinking both ships.

"Freighter. Bearing, mark!"

"Um," Barbara said from the other side of the periscope.

"Give me a bearing."

"Hang on a minute."

Moments passed while the woman tried to read the bearing ring on the periscope shaft.

"Down scope!"

They all jumped as Nixon and his date stomped the floor upstairs, simulating a good depth charging. The destroyer had spotted them.

Percy and Barbara doubled over laughing.

"I thought you knew what you were doing," Charlie said, a little annoyed.

"I'm usually the captain," Barb said.

Charlie reddened. Of course, Percy would give her the role of captain; it was the most gentlemanly thing to do, not to mention the most fun if you considered the whole thing a game. She had a general idea the bearing ring was there but had no idea how to read it.

So much for showing off to a couple of attractive Hawaiian girls. He'd impressed them, all right.

Hang loose, he told himself. Maybe he didn't need to practice anymore but instead honor his promise to himself to let go for one night. Forget the war, have some fun, and start fresh tomorrow.

"Tell Nixon to reset the simulation," he said. "Captain Barb has the conn."

They spent the rest of the night not working but playing, with a little more booze and plenty of laughter.

Meanwhile, Captain Barb took the whole thing quite seriously, sinking an impressive two out of seven ships.

CHAPTER SEVEN

FALSE START

Charlie bounced along in the jeep next to Captain Squadron Commander Rich Cooper, who puffed a cigar and said, "You ready for this, Harrison?"

He thought of Quiet Bill asking him the same question back at PXO School and decided to give the same honest answer. "Is anybody really ready?"

Cooper removed the cigar from his mouth and growled, "Yeah. The men we appoint to command."

"You point me at a Jap ship, and I'll sink it, sir."

"That's what I like to hear," the squadron commander said.

Half the job of being captain was acting like you knew what you were doing.

Cooper parked the jeep on the pier. A Navy band played a rousing circus march at the center of a crowd of well-wishers. The *Sandtiger* lay moored next to the *Harder*, which Captain Harvey's relief crew manned and prepared to sail for a shakedown cruise. Dungareed sailors hustled to complete the loadout.

Charlie braced himself for the usual scathing pep talk about tempering risk with caution, but Cooper only added, "I've got a feeling about you, Harrison."

What kind of feeling, the squadron commander didn't elaborate.

"Yes, sir."

"Find the bastards and sink them. Understand?"

"Aye, aye, sir."

They'd given him only about half the usual complement of torpedoes. They would likely place him outside the Japanese sea lanes. It didn't matter. Excuses didn't matter. Part of the deal in making captain. When he'd taken the conn in previous patrols, he'd had nothing to lose. Now he had everything.

"Good hunting then," the squadron commander said.

Charlie stepped away from the jeep, snapped a salute, and crossed the gangway. He trembled with excitement and anxiety. He'd done this routine act before, but this time, the boat and her crew were under his command.

On the boats, every crewman carried great responsibility. A submarine was a densely packed and complex machine. Just as the failure of a vital piece of equipment could spell disaster, so too could even a small error by one of her crew. Still, the captain bore the ultimate responsibility.

It was enough to make him want to do everything himself, but he knew that wasn't possible. A team sport. He told himself to trust his boat and his crew, one of whom hustled to take his sea bag and stow it in his stateroom.

He mounted to the bridge, where Rusty greeted him with a salute and said, "Welcome aboard, Captain. We'll be able to take her out on time."

Charlie scanned the activity on the main deck. The loadout appeared to be nearing completion. Sailors on the pier coiled the thick hoses by their fuel and water trucks. The torpedo crane stood idle, the weapons hatches secured. The stench of diesel hung in the air, triggering a swirl of emotions.

He glanced up at the *Sandtiger*'s battle flag hanging limp on the jumping wire, a shark in a sailor's hat beside numerous patches, one for each sunken enemy ship. He not only had a responsibility to the Navy and his boat but to Moreau's legacy.

"Torpedoes?" he said.

"Mark 14s. They only gave us one Mark 18."

"Cooper said he expects great things from us."

"Of course he does." Rusty smirked. "You're *Hara-kiri*."

"Oh, brother." The hardest responsibility of all, living up to your own reputation.

Braddock swaggered across the deck leading a train of sailors hauling boxes, the last stores to go down the hatch. "Top of the morning, sir."

"You seem happy to be shoving off, Braddock," Charlie said, not trusting it.

The chief swept his arm across the boxes. "Me and the commissary officer did a little trading and got some beer for the boys."

Percy served as both communications officer as well as commissary officer. He and Braddock could be trouble on their own. Charlie hadn't suspected they might team up to pull a stunt like this.

"And why would you do that?"

"We hand out depth charge medicine after an attack, but we don't give the boys anything but a cake and a turkey dinner after a victory. Give them a can of beer for every ship sunk, and they'll fight like devils. They'll follow you up the River Styx."

Charlie considered it. He glanced at Rusty. "Is it with regulations?"

The exec laughed. "It actually is. The question is where we're going to put it. The boat's packed."

"I'm having some of it put in the officers' shower, sir," Braddock said. "Give you more incentive to sink Jap ships."

Rusty laughed again and shrugged as if to say, *You wanted him, you got him.*

Charlie spied several mailbags in Braddock's train. "And what are those?"

"Newspapers."

A nice morale booster. During idle hours on patrol, the crew would pass the newspapers around and read every word.

"Very well, Chief," Charlie said. "Carry on."

Braddock saluted with an insolent grin and strutted off.

Rusty said, "I think you just brought a hot torpedo aboard."

"As long as he shoots straight."

"That's not what I meant—"

"The men respect him. For all his antics, he respects me. When it matters, he'll be there, and he'll do what needs doing. You can take that to the bank."

Percy bounded up and sketched a salute. "The loadout's complete, Captain. All hands present. Shore power and phone cabling disconnected."

Charlie took in the sight of his communications officer slouching in one of his loud Aloha shirts. "I hope they bring us as much luck as they did Moreau."

The man grinned. "I thought you'd approve."

"If you're smart, you'll push that luck to take things further with Barb."

"You get me back alive, and I might just do that, sir."

Charlie turned to Rusty. "Call the men to quarters."

The crew scrambled to muster on the black deck abaft of the bridge. Within moments, they stood at parade rest, fifty-four enlisted men plus the officers.

He inspected the men, who stared back with expectant half smiles. They appeared rested, spirited, and ready for a fight.

"Buccaneers," he said. "Are you ready to sink ships?"

"AYE, CAPTAIN!"

He nodded to Rusty, who bellowed an order to get to stations.

The *Sandtiger*'s engines rumbled to life, her exhaust vents belching smoke. The band on the pier deftly switched to "Anchors Aweigh" while the crowd cheered and waved. The relief crew on the *Harder* yelled encouragement and ribald insults at Morrison, who raised his clenched fist with a grin. From the *Harder*'s bridge, Captain Harvey glared at Charlie.

"Stand by to single up!" Rusty cried. "Take in

the gangway!" He reported, "Engines have full loading. We can get underway anytime, Captain."

"Very well," Charlie said. "Take us out."

"Single up! Take in two and three! Take in four! Take the strain on one!" The lines piled on the deck. "Take in one!"

Freed from her mooring, the *Sandtiger*'s horn blasted. The engines pulsed with potential energy, shooting vibrations through the deck and bridge coaming. They surged into Charlie and filled him with a fierce sense of power. The *Sandtiger* was a living thing, a wolf smelling blood, and he was a part of her.

The old predator growled as she backed from the pier.

"Helm, all ahead two-thirds," Rusty ordered and broke into a happy smile at the prospect of returning to sea. "Right twenty degrees rudder."

The *Sandtiger* departed from the Submarine Base and dieseled across the busy harbor. Charlie called the men to salute the rusting corpse of the *Arizona*. The submarine navigated the Pearl Harbor Channel and at last found the sea.

The Pacific sprawled before him, a vast magnificent blue, opportunity and the unknown rolled into one, like the future itself.

He gazed upon it with hope and something more. Relief.

The burdens of shore life dropped away, leaving him light and loose. No matter the challenges command and the war might throw at him, life was about to get a whole lot simpler. Charlie was ready to give himself wholeheartedly to his boat and the patrol, ready to grow into his new job and its enormous responsibilities.

As the *Sandtiger* reached from shore, Rusty said, "We're underway, Captain."

"It's good to be back."

First step, a trim dive. The smaller complement of torpedoes and extra gun ammunition had challenged Nixon to distribute the load in proper balance. The dive would reveal any deficiencies.

"Bridge, Conn," Nixon said over the bridge loudspeaker.

"This is the captain," Charlie responded.

"The radio isn't working, sir. We can't receive messages."

"Why isn't it working?"

Nixon launched into a long technical description of the problem until Charlie cut in, "How long until you can get it repaired?"

"That's the thing. We're missing a part. It isn't in the inventory."

"Can you jury-rig something?"

Nixon hesitated. Charlie sensed the man was embarrassed. "Not for this problem, Captain."

"Then…"

"We either have to go back for it," Rusty said with disgust, "or make the run to Midway without a working radio."

Charlie's fists clenched, but there was nothing to hit, nothing for him to do other than take this punch like a man.

He turned to Rusty. "Suggestions?"

"I laid out our options. They're both shit."

His stomach sank. Within an hour of getting underway, he had to bring his boat back to port with its tail between its legs. Embarrassing. He told himself these things happened, but it was a bad start for his first patrol as captain.

"Very well. Conn, Bridge. Left full rudder. We're going to come about and return to base. And Nixon?"

"Aye, Captain?"

"Between now and our return, check everything. We're only doing this once."

"Aye, aye."

The *Sandtiger* completed her ponderous turn and cruised back into the Pearl Harbor Channel. A submarine was coming their way.

The *Harder*, manned by Captain Harvey and his crew.

"He's flashing a signal," Rusty said.

"An apology for leaving us with a non-working radio, maybe," Charlie said.

The submarines drew close to each other. Captain Harvey stood motionless on the bridge while his sailors waved. A blinker gun flashed a message in Morse code.

Charlie's fists clenched again.

The message was, FORGET SOMETHING?

CHAPTER EIGHT

MIDWAY

In the sweltering after engine room, Chief Machinist John Braddock crossed his hairy arms over his barrel chest. Now, he wore a peaked cap on his big head. While the officers and crew didn't wear hats during a patrol, the chiefs often did to designate their status.

"Saltwater," he shouted over the throbbing engines. "In the reduction gears."

Charlie scoured his memory of the boat's systems. "A leak between the bilges and the sumps?"

The bilge was the space where the submarine's bottom curved to join its vertical sides. Any water in the boat drained there until it was pumped out. The sump was the base of the engine, serving as a reservoir for lubricating oil.

"We checked out the tank tops but didn't see anything."

"Did you test the oil coolers?" Nixon said.

Braddock tilted his head to signal he'd obviously done that. He'd take such a question from the captain but nobody else.

Nixon didn't seem to notice. "How do the gears look?"

Charlie braced himself for bad news. The boat's reduction gears allowed a decrease in output speed while maintaining the same rotational force, or torque. This very simple function enabled propulsion.

The four main diesel engines drove four generators, which produced electric power to operate four motors. The motors drove the boat's two propellers using reduction gears that lowered input speed from 1,300 rotations per minute to the 280 RPMs the propellers required.

"A little rust," Braddock said. "But no pitting. They're good."

"Inspect the oil sumps and take samples daily," Nixon said.

The chief glanced at Charlie, who nodded.

"Aye, aye, Mr. Nixon," Braddock said.

Charlie sighed. They'd had nothing but trouble since leaving Pearl Harbor five days ago. Unless ground in, the exhaust valves allowed water into the engine room bilges, which had to be pumped out or the engines would flood. A fuel oil leak from a damaged injector jumper line on the No. 2 main engine diluted the after sump, requiring a complete replacement of the lubricating oil. Then the connecting rod bearing of a unit in the auxiliary engine wiped, scoring the crankshaft.

Problems like these were common enough on the submarines, due to defect, faulty installation, wear and tear, or battle damage. They weren't supposed to happen this frequently and so soon after refitting.

"I'm starting to think that relief crew sabotaged us," Nixon said.

"The boat's past her prime," Braddock said. "She got rattled one too many times scrapping with the Japs." He patted the nearest engine humming on its mount. "The uglier she gets, the more love she needs."

"There's a submarine tender at Midway. We should give her a thorough check."

Charlie glanced at Braddock, who shook his head.

Aside from staring at gooney birds, Midway offered no amusements. Submarine crews hated going on liberty there, preferring the fleshpots of Honolulu. They'd rather do drills than end up idle at the base. Charlie intended to stay as briefly as possible so he could get the *Sandtiger* into her patrol area on schedule.

"Can you keep her in fighting trim?" he asked.

The chief wiped his oily hands on a rag. "Yup. She'll hold."

"We can't afford any more delay."

"The crew thanks you, sir."

"All right," he said. "Check the inventory. If this is how it's going to be on this patrol, we'll need plenty of spare parts. Tell Mr. Nixon what you need before we reach Midway."

"Aye, aye," Braddock said and added, "sir."

A call from the conn came through on the 7MC. He picked up the sound-powered phone. "This is the captain."

"How bad is it?" Rusty asked him.

"It's like we're back on Frankie."

The first boat on which he'd served with Rusty, the S-55, had been a broken-down sewer pipe, fickle and barely seaworthy. Battered and scarred, she'd held together long enough to get them home after one more good fight.

Rusty snorted. "I remember that patrol well. You fought the Japs, while I fought Frankie. I just wanted to report we've made landfall."

At least the radar was working and they'd found Midway, which, being as small as it was, actually wasn't an easy task. *If nothing else*, Charlie thought, *I got that right.*

He stepped out of the engine compartment

and mounted to the conning tower. "Take us in, Rusty. I'm going to the bridge."

"Wait." His friend approached and added, "You look really wound up. You find out something's wrong with the boat?"

"It's what I didn't find that worries me," Charlie said. "Nothing seems to be going right on this patrol, and it's barely even started. I feel like I'm waiting for the next sucker punch."

Rusty relaxed. "That's just first-command jitters. Try and take it easy. You can only deal with what you know. The rest will take care of itself."

"I'm still getting my sea legs on this job." He started for the ladder and stopped with a self-deprecating chuckle. "You know, I got a letter from Evie just before we shoved off. She was worried about me. Said she had a dream I was drowning. I think she meant this job."

"Must have been that," Rusty said, clearly rattled.

"What's with…? Oh, come on."

"Did Percy tell you about his dream where he goes home, and his family tells him he died in the war?"

"It's just a dream."

"Yeah, everybody keeps dreaming we're going to die."

"How can you be so superstitious?"

"You're in the Navy. How can you not be?"

"I can only deal with what's in front of me—ah, okay." Charlie laughed. "Well, that got my head on straight. Thanks for the talk, Rusty."

"Anytime," Rusty said, still looking pale. "Sure thing."

Charlie mounted to the bridge. Seabirds shrieked in a bright blue sky as the *Sandtiger* cruised toward the Midway Atoll. Roughly equidistant between North America and Asia, and one-third of the way between Pearl and Tokyo, Midway was a chain of islands, coral reef, and seamounts.

Before the war, the Navy considered it second only to Pearl in strategic importance and built an air station there. Since then, it had become a major base. Landfilling had doubled Sand Island's size, and it was now home to a second airfield as well as a tender and floating dry dock servicing submarines.

There, the *Sandtiger* would top her fuel tanks, pick up mail, and take on fresh stores. And most important, Charlie thought with a smile, he'd be able to open his sealed operation order, which would reveal his first war patrol as captain.

An albatross cried and dive-bombed the submarine, dropping a turd that splatted on the bridge deck.

Charlie frowned. Maybe somebody was trying to tell him something. He didn't hold with superstition, but he was starting to see its merits.

CHAPTER NINE

AREA TWENTY

The *Sandtiger* reached from Midway, plowing through calm sea on three mains. In the wardroom, Charlie and his officers gathered around the small table while Waldron, the steward, poured coffee all around.

Percy flapped his Aloha shirt against his sweating chest. "Is it me, or is the boat hot as hell?"

"We had a failure in the air conditioning," Nixon said. "The A-gang is on it."

"It makes you wonder if the boat's haunted."

Rusty's eyes widened. "Will you guys stop saying stuff like that?"

The communications officer grinned. "Vengeful spirits, Exec. All those Japs we killed? There's a legend—"

"Gentlemen." Charlie held up an envelope, its seal broken. "Our operation order."

The men silenced to listen. Nixon slurped his

coffee. Percy lit a cigarette and squinted behind a cloud of silver smoke.

He read, "One, sink Japanese shipping."

The men smiled. Sinking enemy ships was a standing order in the submarines.

"Two, we'll be doing that in Area Twenty, which is the good news." Charlie spread a chart on the table. "It's a stretch of water off the east coast of the Philippines." He tapped it. "Covering Samar Island to about here." In terms of area, Area Twenty was about the size of New Jersey.

No major shipping lanes, which were to the west, but they'd expected that. Still, the patrol area straddled minor sea lanes between Manila and Peleliu, which was under assault by the U.S. Marines, and between Manila and Davao on Mindanao Island.

Legend had it the Spanish explorers who'd first arrived at Samar found a wounded man and asked him the name of the island. Not understanding Spanish, the man answered, "*samad*," which meant "cut" or "wound."

"We might bag a troopship heading for Peleliu," Charlie added. "Maybe some trawlers and coasters in the local traffic."

Morrison perked up. "Sounds like a job for my commandos."

Charlie nodded. "Three, we're going to monitor the area for enemy warships. If we see any, we're not to engage. We're to radio it in. ComSubPac also wants us to take intelligence photos along the coast."

Other submarines were on station surrounding the islands. ComSubPac intended to throttle the Philippines.

"That's not a bad first patrol for you, Captain," Percy said.

"With ten lousy torpedoes, we'll have to make every shot count," Rusty said.

"On the plus side," Morrison pointed out, "we're almost guaranteed a clean sweep."

"Now that we're past Midway, there's something I need to tell you about this patrol," Charlie said. "Or rather, Nixon will. Tell them about the secret weapon."

"Secret weapon?" Morrison's eyes lit up. "I like it already."

"Defensive measure, really," Nixon said. "I'm sure you're all familiar with the *Pillenwerfer* and the *Sieglinde*."

The men returned blank stares, which Charlie didn't find surprising. The Americans fighting across the Pacific were jealous about their side of the war, largely unaware of what was happening in the European theater. Charlie himself only just learned the Allies had liberated Paris after reading one of the newspapers Braddock brought aboard.

"Come on, guys," Nixon huffed. "You need to keep up with the scuttlebutt."

"Fill them in," Charlie said.

"The Germans developed two countermeasures we were able to copy. The *Pillenwerfer*, which means 'pill thrower,' is a metal can filled with calcium hydride. Seawater reacts with it and makes a huge amount of hydrogen, which bubbles out of the can."

"And the Japs bomb the bubbles instead of us," Percy said. "Sweet cherry pie."

Rusty said, "How long does it last?"

"Twenty minutes, supposedly," Nixon told him. "Maybe twenty-five."

"What's the other upgrade?"

"The *Sieglinde*, which is Kraut for 'shield.' It's a straight-up sonar decoy. We shoot it from the sides of the boat. Electric motors keep it going at a speed of six knots, and rise and fall in depth. On sonar, it sounds just like a submarine."

"While we make tracks on silent running." Percy's face glowed like a kid given a shiny new toy. "I'm so happy."

Like all submariners, he hated being depth charged. While Japanese depth charging was largely ineffective except in shallow waters, that didn't stop it from being terrifying. The only way Charlie could describe it was like being on the ground floor of a collapsing building.

"It's brand new," he said. "We were lucky to be in refitting when the first arrived. We're one of the only boats in the entire Pacific to have it."

Rusty shrugged. "I'll love it if it works. The Navy still can't make a decent torpedo."

The Navy had finally acknowledged and fixed the problems with the Mark 14 and then put out the new and improved Mark 18, a wakeless torpedo. Still, one out of three shots fired was a dud or went erratic in the water. Some went on terrifying circular runs, putting the submarine at risk of sinking itself.

"Ideally, we won't need to use them at all," Charlie pointed out. "It's insurance, there if we need it. By the time we reach Area Twenty, we'll need to have the crew properly trained on the procedures. Nixon, see to it."

"Aye, Captain."

The meeting broke up soon after that. Rusty returned to his duties while Percy and Nixon headed for some rack time. Charlie sat alone, drinking his coffee and feeling a solid deck under his feet for the first time since the patrol started.

Evie's dream, a seabird dropping a fecal bomb on his deck, getting stiffed on torpedoes, the patrol's false start, the boat's systems going broke dick one by one—bad omens, maybe, but none of it mattered anymore. The operation order was good news. Area Twenty offered solid hunting prospects.

Frequent drills, the firehose treatment for the greenhorns, and a return to old routines and the usual school-of-the-boat were whipping the crew into shape. By the time the *Sandtiger* got on station, they'd fuse into a well-oiled machine. And they had the latest countermeasures that would protect them if they were detected.

In the waters off Samar, Charlie planned to raise hell wherever any opportunity presented itself.

The general alarm bleated, accompanied by a clanging bell. He sprang to his feet.

Rusty's voice blared over the 1MC: "Fire in aft torpedo!"

CHAPTER TEN

JINXED

The *Sandtiger* dieseled southwest by west on choppy seas 2,200 nautical miles from Midway, getting a solid radar fix on landmasses within range. They'd reached the Marianas.

On the bridge with their legs braced wide against the boat's pitch, Charlie and Rusty studied Saipan with binoculars.

Relatively quiet except for some holdouts still fighting in the jungles, the island was a smudge on the horizon. With its capture, America had struck a vital blow against the Japanese Empire. Tokyo was now within distance of B-29 Superfortress bombers, which regularly pounded the Japanese mainland and the Philippines. The disaster had forced Prime Minister Hideki Tojo to resign.

The beginning of the end.

The submarine cruised onward until the island's hazy outline bled into the big blue, taking with it all reminiscence about bayonet charges,

Alamo Scouts, Smokey's sacrifice, and Jane's comforting touch.

The war would end soon. As much as Charlie wanted that, he longed to prove himself as captain. As many patrols as he could get.

"We'll be on station the morning after tomorrow," Rusty noted.

"Then we'll deep six this jinx," said Charlie. "You'll see."

Rusty's superstition had started to infect him. Whether the boat was jinxed or not didn't matter. Too many things were going wrong.

From the captain's log, four days earlier:

September 22, 1944

1150   Moored starboard side to MIDWAY fuel dock. Took on fuel, some stores, and spare parts.

1412   Underway for patrol area.

1531   Explosion in #8 torpedo tube, producing heavy, white, sulfurous smoke out vent and petcocks. Removed torpedo from the tube and examined it. Smoke necessitated evacuating Aft Torpedo while ventilating at full blower speed.

1555   Fire in torpedo battery compartment. Heavy smoke necessitated breathing apparatus while fire controlled using CO_2 extinguishers. Torpedo disabled and stored for salvage.

Even now, the boat still stank like sulfur, and headaches were common. Meanwhile, the *Sandtiger* had one less torpedo to take on patrol. Another sucker punch Charlie hadn't seen coming.

Braddock mounted to the bridge, which could only mean further troubles in the boat. "A word, sir?"

Charlie stifled a groan. "What's the problem?"

Braddock glanced at the lookouts perched on the shears and lowered his voice. "You, sir."

"Me?"

"You need to let go of this jinx business. You're drinking too much coffee and riding the department heads."

"If any of these problems happened in combat, we'd have been in big trouble. We need to be ready for anything."

Rusty said, "The captain's right. Every couple of hours, it seems—"

"And you, Exec! Harrison here is letting the boat's aches stand in for his doubts about command. You're supposed to know better. This old girl got herself punched in the face about ten too many times. It's that simple."

It was a fair point. In just her last two war patrols, the *Sandtiger* had logged 18,000 miles and had survived multiple, brutal depth-charge attacks, not to mention a hot torpedo exploding close aboard.

"Thank you for speaking up," Charlie said, remembering he'd risked bringing the man along so he'd always hear it straight. "But I don't believe in jinxes. I'm just worried about the boat. We'll be in combat soon."

"Great. Fine. It doesn't matter. The crew looks to you guys to see how to act. Right now, some of them are starting to come down with the heebie-jeebies."

Charlie and Rusty exchanged a glance. Braddock was a pain in the ass, but he was an old sea dog. The man had a solid point.

"We'll set the right example," Charlie said.

Braddock grinned. "I already took care of them, sir. One of my snipes writes his wife every day and even sends love poems. The wives back home

72

keep in touch, see, and they're none too happy about how often their men write *them*. I've got every married A-ganger writing poetry when they're off duty."

Rusty laughed then groaned. "I'm going to have to read and censor all their letters before posting to mail. Get us into action quick, Skipper. A flattop, a battle group, even the goddamn *Yamato*. Quick, before they finish writing them."

Charlie laughed too. Braddock was turning into one hell of a morale officer. "Thank you, Chief. Carry on."

The sailor touched his knuckle to his forehead in a rough salute. "Anytime, sir." He climbed back down the hatch.

"As much as I hate him for doing that," Rusty said, "I have to admit you made the right call bringing him aboard."

"Smokey always had the temper of the men," Charlie explained. "And I could always rely on him to tell it like it is. I expected the same of Braddock. So far, he hasn't disappointed me."

"He's like a new man." The exec sighed. "So no more jinx talk."

Which meant no talking about it and no fretting either.

Easier said than done for Charlie, with whom the buck stopped as captain. Cooper had assigned him a patrol area with fair hunting prospects. While the squadron commander would read Charlie's patrol report and sympathize with his problems, they were *his* problems. The Navy expected results.

It triggered his instinct to try to control everything, including the things he couldn't control. The less he could, the more things went wrong under his command, the more he doubted himself.

He reminded himself he'd been in this situation before and with much bigger stakes. After his last patrol to the Philippines during which he'd modified his torpedoes, he'd expected never to set foot on a submarine again. In the Sea of Japan, he'd crossed Moreau, the last man you'd ever want to cross, and expected banishment to a desk job for the remainder of the war. During his patrol to Saipan, Saunders had accused him of mutiny and planned to court-martial him.

Each time, he'd fought as hard as he could until his options ran out. Then he'd decided to take his punch and let the chips fall where they did. He had to do the same now. He had to let go.

He'd never been good at doing that. He didn't want to let go, knowing his self-doubt, plus the fact he was wound a bit tight, made him a good officer. But he'd always been a fast learner, and it was time to learn. If he didn't, he might end up like Saunders, a man worn down until broken by the pressures of command, or Bob Hunter, who blamed himself for his faulty torpedoes.

The *Sandtiger* was showing her age and wounds, but she remained a wolf. If any problems surfaced, his capable crew had his back. He had to trust them both and work on being the best commander he could be, and that started with setting the right example in every respect.

"No more jinx talk," Charlie agreed.

CHAPTER ELEVEN

SAMAR

Samar was the Philippines' third largest island. To the northwest was Luzon, the largest in the archipelago. To the south, Leyte and Leyte Gulf. To the east, the Philippine Sea, the *Sandtiger*'s patrol area.

She ranged fifteen miles off the coast, hunting.

Plenty of fishing boats, piloted by locals. Frequent Japanese patrol planes. A PT boat hugging the coast. Otherwise, nothing.

Two more days passed, and still nothing.

Then two weeks. Then another, without spotting even a single puff of smoke.

One could say the jinx continued.

In the conning tower, Charlie raised the observation periscope. He doubted this dry spell had anything to do with bad luck. Instead, it proved the powerful capability of America's growing submarine fleet.

There were far fewer Japanese merchantmen than there were just a year ago, while the Navy added a new submarine to the Submarine Force every week.

The *Sandtiger* had at last worked out her kinks and appeared ready for a fight. The air conditioning continued to struggle, unable to cool the boat lower than a balmy ninety degrees. Otherwise, her systems performed well, and Charlie was confident about taking her into combat.

As for her crew, they were getting restless, but he'd taken the opportunity to drill and school them. Almost every sailor aboard was getting extra training, and even the greenhorns, working their way through their notebooks for qualification, looked good. Charlie and Rusty had interviewed many of the department heads and crewmen, searching for even minor modifications that would improve efficiency. To keep them entertained, Charlie had ordered the radioman to play popular records during the dog watch hours when the crew ate their evening meals. While they hadn't seen action yet, the men were sharp.

Like the boat, the crew had settled into a solid rhythm. Now he just had to get them a target. Finding ships they could sink was his job and his alone. He visited the radioman daily to remind him to bring any Ultra messages from Pearl straight to him, day or night. Every day, he prayed for one of these burn messages advising of a big, juicy convoy coming his way, but none arrived.

He swiveled the periscope, taking in the black mass of Samar with its hills and mountainous terrain, their steep slopes bare of trees. Rain ran off these inclines, carrying topsoil that enlarged the coastal planes, mudflats, and mangrove swamps.

Nothing. Not even a plane.

"Down scope," he said. "Let's look at the chart."

Having benefitted more than once from chance, Charlie understood the role of luck in war but didn't see it as anything being superstitious could influence. He believed in making your own luck through smart planning.

Time to find some trouble.

"One chart, coming right up," Percy said with genuine cheer.

The communications officer didn't seem to mind the heat, and the lack of action suited him just fine. The war would end soon. Everybody felt it. The stronger that feeling, the more they thought about home and making it back alive.

Percy spread the chart on the plotting table. An American chart, recently updated. Using it,

Charlie could conn the boat close to shore without fear of running her aground or into a reef. Still, navigation would be challenging, and there was a greater risk of running into a mine.

Morrison joined them, glancing from the chart to Charlie's face with eagerness. Guys like him, they weren't going back until they'd done something.

As for Charlie, he wasn't until he'd done all he could.

He studied the coastline and settled on a town nestled on the island's southeastern coast. A small fishing town of no real strategic importance, facing Matarinao Bay. Its name was Hernani, population around 6,000.

"Percy, give me a course for this town," he said. "I want to get us close enough for observation and possible action tonight."

Percy gave him a curious stare then shrugged. "Aye, Captain."

Morrison seethed, knowing he shouldn't question his captain, but finally unable to stop himself. "Why there, sir?"

Because Charlie hadn't seen any Japanese ships in twenty-one days, and he needed to roll the dice. Because the Japanese were likely using coasters, small cargo ships that hugged the shore, to avoid submarines. Because after their occupation of the Philippines, the enemy might have built up Hernani as an anchorage for these vessels.

"Call it a hunch," Charlie said with a cryptic smile.

Morrison grinned. When *Hara-kiri* had a hunch, it likely meant action was afoot. "Say the word, Captain, and we'll be ready to play."

Frequent drills had made the lieutenant's gun crew razor sharp, and he'd practiced tactics with his commando assault team. They were another of the boat's secret weapons.

Charlie scowled, however, irritated at himself playing it up for the eager officer who idolized him. The truth was he had nothing else to go on, and he was done waiting for the enemy to come to him.

Meanwhile, time was running out. This morning, the sunrise had been a fiery scarlet. A buildup of water vapor in the atmosphere, scattering short-wavelength light. That meant a big storm was on the way, which would hinder detection of enemy ships and waste time.

"Very well," he growled. "Return to your duties."

"Aye, aye, Captain."

Percy said, "Recommend a course of two-oh-five."

"Helm, come left to new course, two-oh-five," Charlie ordered.

Not much to do now but wait, something he'd had plenty of practice doing during his time in the submarines.

By late morning, the *Sandtiger* approached the entrance to Matarinao Bay.

"I'm picking up fast, light screws," the soundman reported. "Bearing, two-one-oh."

Charlie suppressed a sigh of relief, playing it cool. "Very well. Up scope."

He crouched as the periscope whirred from its well. He rose with it, yanking the handles down. Face pressed against the rubber eyepiece, he circled several times, carefully scanning the sky for planes. Then he settled on the ship.

"He's a DE," he announced. "*Matsu* class."

A destroyer escort, what the British called a frigate. A recent addition to the Imperial Japanese Navy's new Grand Escort Fleet. Lighter and smaller than previous designs, cheap and simplified for fast construction, but fitted with enhanced anti-submarine and AA weaponry. A sub killer.

Charlie's lips parted in a predatory smile. His hunch was correct. The IJN had designed the *Matsu* for one purpose, which was protecting merchantmen. A DE on sentry duty at the mouth of a bay? Cargo ships were very likely stopping at Hernani.

The sleek escort paced, its knuckle bow slicing the water. The water behind it was red like blood, the result of a runaway algal bloom, what sailors called a "red tide." It killed the fish and could even make the air difficult to breathe.

"Down scope," he said.

The scope withdrew. Morrison stared at him with wide eyes. Charlie looked away, gratified and irritated. He needed to think without having any expectations pressed on him from the Navy, his crew, and least of all Morrison.

Attack or wait?

He wanted to get closer to spot the ships this escort guarded but thought better of it. The entrance to the bay was only two and a half miles across, and Anahap Island blocked his view from the sea.

He approached the plotting table, where Percy tracked the ship's movements based on sound bearings.

Back and forth went the warship.

The submarine's natural enemy, a destroyer always made a risky target. They were fast, had a shallow draft, and could find you with echo ranging and pound you with depth charges if you missed. Shallow water played hell with sonar. However, there would be no thermals or depths in which to hide, and it allowed the possibility of detection with the naked eye, and depth charging was much more likely to disable or destroy a submarine.

Right now, the *Sandtiger* had only 120 feet under her keel. Little room to maneuver.

On the other hand, if Charlie sank this *Matsu*, whatever ships it was guarding at Hernani would be sitting ducks for the *Sandtiger*'s weaponry. He'd wreak havoc. What a statement that would make on his first patrol!

Charlie thought about it further while Morrison bounced on his heels. Even the rest of his crew shot him inquisitive glances. With the *Sandtiger* carrying less than half her usual complement of torpedoes, he wanted to shoot them at cargo ships, not escorts, which were very low-value targets. It might take only one or two torpedoes to sink the *Matsu*, but for insurance, he'd have to shoot at least three, ideally four. An alert lookout might spot the torpedo wakes. The speedy *Matsu* could then evade, and Charlie would have shot his wad for nothing. He could throw his single Mark 18 on a wing and a prayer. Being wakeless, the escort wouldn't see the torpedo until it blew a hole in the ship's hull. But Charlie didn't have faith in it working properly. Back to square one.

If only he could see what this destroyer was guarding. There might be a particularly tasty target, like an oil tanker, hiding behind

Anahap. Or there might be more warships ready to clobber him.

Captain Moreau, the poker player, would probably attack, betting the pot was worth it. *The enemy is there*, he'd say, *so that's where we'll hit him*. With a storm on the way, he'd see it as his best bet. Attack now, and go all in.

Captain Kane, the chess player, would pass on a good move until he'd fully considered whether a better one was in the offing. As commander of an old broken-down sugar boat, Kane had understood how to work with his limitations.

As a lieutenant, Charlie had wondered what it was like to stand in their shoes. Submarine captains were expected to produce results while streaming a constant calculus of risk and reward. Now he knew. The pressure was enormous, a crushing weight as heavy and real as the sea during a deep dive.

Attacking would be hard, waiting even harder. Then again, he'd always been better at chess than poker. He knew how to be patient.

Whatever ships were hiding behind Anahap, they wouldn't stay long. When they put to sea, he'd be able to pick his target and spend his torpedoes wisely.

Praying the storm held off a while longer, he decided to wait.

CHAPTER TWELVE

CONTACT

The *Sandtiger* prowled offshore, waiting, until the soundman called out the destroyer escort had changed course.

Heading straight for the *Sandtiger*.

Another set of light screws. And one set of heavy screws.

Charlie ordered the helmsman to come left until his submarine's bow pointed at the enemy. That way, he could raise his periscope with an almost undetectable feather in the water.

While submerged, the soundman was the boat's ears, but Charlie was her eyes.

"All ahead one-third," he said, fighting his rising excitement. Heavy screws meant a large warship or more likely a merchantman. "Up scope."

A year ago, he might have thought it strange to find two escorts guarding a *maru*, but not now. For him, it was just more evidence the submarines had taken a massive toll on the empire's merchant fleet.

He suppressed a smile, forcing an expression of sullen competence. He had to act as if his hunch had been more than a desperate shot in the dark. That he'd planned all this, and finding ships here was not just a happy surprise.

Was it like this for Moreau? He'd always appeared to know what he was doing, where the enemy was. For that bloodhound to find a target, all he had to do was sniff hard enough.

The attack periscope rose above the surface. Charlie circled to scan for planes before settling his view on the menacing V shape of a Japanese destroyer.

The sea and island backdrop were still as a photograph, the result of the coming storm front pulling warm, moist air into itself and pushing it back out as stable, dry air.

The literal calm before the storm.

Hugging the periscope, he shifted the view until he found the second escort. He called out bearings for Percy to mark on the plot. With careful tracking, Charlie would have a future route into the bay past any mines.

At last, into view came the prize, the ship the DEs were guarding.

At first glance, he thought it was an oiler. Then he recalled its profile from the reference book.

"Down scope." He stepped back from the withdrawing periscope and smiled at his crew. "Gentlemen, we found the *Mamiya*."

A large food transport ship, 15,000 tons. It carried enough food to provision an entire division for nearly a month.

"I thought he'd been sunk by the *Cero* almost a year ago," Percy said.

"No, it was the *Spearfish*, I heard," Morrison chimed in.

Charlie shrugged. On two separate occasions, these submarines had apparently damaged but not sunk the ship. "This time, it'll be the *Sandtiger*, and we'll be putting him down for good."

He ran his hand over his stubbled face. The enemy cruised single file on a 195° True bearing, but that would likely change any second as the group exited the bay and chose its course. Likely to Peleliu to resupply the troops fighting there, or return to Japan. Either way, Charlie had him in the bag.

The *Sandtiger* held course at the center of the bay's entrance. No matter where the *maru* went, Charlie would have a shot.

The question was whether he wanted to attack now or wait.

If he attacked, he'd have to fire a spread. The Mark 14s would leave a trail of backwash leading directly to the *Sandtiger*. The escorts would be on top of her in minutes and pound her with depth charges.

Charlie didn't want to bet on the new countermeasures unless he had no choice, but if he attacked in those shallow waters, he'd likely have to use them.

The other option was to plot the enemy's base course, wait until they'd gone over the hill, and then do an end-around. Go in hard and fast on the surface, under cover of darkness before moonrise, and sink the bastard. Charlie might even get two shots at the target, allowing him the possibility of conserving torpedoes. He preferred this type of submarine combat, quick and mobile.

The only problem was the storm. If it hit while the *Sandtiger* pursued her prey, she might lose contact altogether.

The men watched him as he thought it all out. Taut and expectant faces glistening with sweat and sprouting new beards. They wore diesel-stained shorts and sandals. Already starting to look like proper pirates.

"Battle stations, torpedo attack," he said.

The alarm sounded throughout the boat. Hands rushed to quarters.

In the end, he didn't have that much of a choice. He had the *maru* in the bag and didn't want to risk losing it later.

"Target is a food transport, bearing oh-four-oh," Charlie called out. "Range, about 6,000 yards. Give him thirteen knots."

Standing at the TDC, located aft to port, Morrison adjusted a series of knobs, entering these variables into the computer. Using the boat's instruments, the crew would fine-tune the numbers until the TDC produced an accurate firing solution.

"Two escorts screening," Charlie added, providing a complete picture. "*Matsu*-class DEs. Sound, keep those bearings coming."

His senses tingled. The *Sandtiger* hummed all around him. She'd had her breakdowns, but now, he hoped, she'd deliver when it counted.

Bleary from sleep and still buttoning the shirt of his service khakis, Rusty mounted to the conning tower. "I'm here!"

The telephone talker said, "All compartments report battle stations manned, Captain. The crew is at general quarters."

"Very well. Up scope."

Charlie crouched and rose with the periscope, slapping its handles into place. The sea was calm as a sheet of glass. The *maru*'s dark gray hull plowed the water, its single funnel belching smoke.

His eyes roamed across the superstructure, the gun platforms on both the bow and stern, the derricks protruding next to the cargo holds.

"Food transport," he said. "Mark the bearing."

Rusty called out the bearing ring reading on the other side of the periscope shaft. Morrison fed the number into the TDC.

"Range, mark!" Charlie said.

"Range, 5,000 yards!" Rusty answered. "Angle on the bow, starboard forty and opening."

"Down scope."

When the angle on the bow reached ninety degrees, the *Sandtiger* would be facing the target's broadside.

The ideal time to fire.

CHAPTER THIRTEEN

WINDOW OF OPPORTUNITY

Charlie studied the tactical picture portrayed on the plotting table. The enemy ships steamed as close to the coast as they dared, the *Mamiya* with land to port. The escorts held station off the *maru's* starboard bow and quarter.

After Percy confirmed the target's speed, Charlie had enough information to determine an approach and firing position. He'd come about and shoot his wad from the stern tubes. By firing from the stern, the boat would be in good position for escaping to the deeper waters of the open sea.

"Helm, right full rudder," he ordered.

The helmsman, who steered the boat at his station mounted against the forward bulkhead, repeated the order and turned the rudder hard over.

After the turn put him on the desired bearing, Charlie said, "Rudder amidships."

"Rudder amidships, aye, Captain," the helmsman answered.

Aside from routine chatter, the men remained quiet, focused on their tasks in the excited atmosphere. Charlie found himself with time to double-check his approach and attack plan. During the long wait before firing torpedoes, many captains second-guessed themselves into failure, but not him. The setup was less complicated than many problems he'd encountered in the attack trainer. Only 2,500 yards from the target's track, which he'd easily close to 1,500 in time to shoot his fish.

He scanned the cramped conning tower jammed with ten men sweating in the stale, humid air. A few stared back with wide eyes. He smiled, hoping it conveyed confidence and not the mix of anxiety and childish excitement he felt. Percy returned a glum expression, resigned to his fate. Morrison grinned at the TDC.

Rusty regarded him with his face screwed up in thought, probably wondering if Charlie had thought the whole thing through or was rushing to the attack to prove himself. "You know, those escorts are going to clobber us."

"Probably," Charlie said. "Up scope."

The periscope broke the surface. The targets were larger now, coming on fast.

"Bearing, mark!"

Rusty called it out for Morrison.

Range, closing. Speed unchanged at thirteen knots. Angle on the bow, starboard seventy and continuing to widen.

"This will be a stern shot," Charlie said.

He conned the boat to come about so his stern faced the enemy.

"We get depth charged in these shallow waters, we'll be feeling it," Rusty said.

"Noted," Charlie replied, in no mood for a debate. "Target is the *Mamiya*. We'll fire three fish from 1,500 yards." He'd wanted to fire a fourth for insurance, but the faulty torpedo had been removed. "Aft Torpedo, make ready the stern tubes."

He felt a thud as the outer doors opened.

"Stern tubes ready, Captain," the telephone talker said.

"Very well. Order of tubes is one, two, three. High speed, depth eight feet. Up scope!" Charlie centered the crosshairs under the *maru*'s smoking funnel. "He's coming on. Aft Torpedo, stand by. Final bearing, mark!"

Rusty: "Oh-four-three!"

"Range, mark!"

"Sixteen hundred yards!"

The men tensed, waiting for the order to fire. The conning tower went dead quiet as seconds ticked by.

At 1,500 yards, he'd—

The soundman called out, "Captain! The escorts are—"

"I see it," Charlie said in surprise.

The escorts had rapidly shifted position, the lead escort slowing while the rear escort accelerated, a risky and delicate maneuver they'd obviously practiced. Together, they formed a wall blocking the *Mamiya*.

Charlie didn't believe they'd spotted his periscope and were taking defensive action. He'd heard of Japanese skippers doing crazy maneuvers to throw off submarines. It was just his bum luck they'd done it while he was attacking.

Regardless, the question remained. Should he fire his torpedoes?

He still had a firing solution. If he hit one of the escorts, he'd at least have gained something, though the Navy would consider it more a waste of a good torpedo than a big win. If the torpedoes passed under them, or if the ships dodged out of the way, he might still hit the *maru*.

Or he might miss, shooting partially blind, and take a beating for nothing.

The risks had substantially increased with this curveball. So did the angle on the bow. With each passing second, his window of opportunity closed quickly.

If he passed on the attack, he could do an end-around and take another shot later in open, deeper sea. He hated the idea of letting go, though. The men were counting on him. Cooper and ComSubPac were counting on him. His blood was up. He was itching for combat.

No time to think it through. Too late now to do anything.

The firing solution light winked off at the TDC.

"Check fire," Morrison said.

"Down scope," he said with disgust. "We're standing down. Abort attack. Secure the tubes. Secure from battle stations."

In the end, he just couldn't risk it. The *Mamiya* was too important a target to stage an attack lacking in certainty. He needed to focus on that ship and sink it.

Across the conning tower, the crewmen blew out a collective sigh. Of relief or frustration, Charlie didn't know. Morrison stared in disbelief.

"What happened?" Rusty said.

"The escorts changed it up and walled off the target," Charlie fumed. With the target's speed and an angle on the bow widening from ninety, the *Sandtiger* couldn't hope to catch up and line up another shot. "We're going to wait and start an end-around."

"We'll get him tonight," Rusty assured him.

The concern in his friend's voice, touched with pity, only made Charlie feel worse.

CHAPTER FOURTEEN

A GOOD COMMANDER

The *Sandtiger* lunged from the sea as the last Japanese ship went over the hill.

Charlie, Rusty, and Chief Jack Hooker, on duty as quartermaster of the watch, mounted to the bridge. The usual three lookouts scrambled up the shears. Another two lookouts took positions on the bridge and cigarette deck, keeping a careful eye out for enemy planes.

Charlie had surfaced the boat to make a run in daylight, though thunderheads gloomed on the eastern horizon. The coming storm would make his hunt a lot harder, but he hoped it would also keep enemy patrol planes on the ground. Until then, the roughening seas would hide the *Sandtiger*'s wake, making the submarine more difficult to spot from the air.

Below deck, the electricians uncoupled the electric motors from the batteries and connected them to the diesels. The submarine trembled as the engines fired and breathed smoke. She made way east by northeast on two mains while the other engines dumped amps into the depleted batteries. Once the batteries charged, Charlie planned to open up with all four mains.

As they departed the area, the targets had zigzagged, including a new pattern he'd never seen before and appeared random. Percy had their northerly base course pegged, however. The ships were likely heading to Taiwan, though they might slip west into the San Bernardino Strait between Samar and Luzon for a run to Manila.

He hoped that, by moving quickly, he could get ahead of them before they reached Luzon. Though he had to circle around just over the horizon, he had the faster ship, and zigzagging slowed the enemy down. If any Japanese planes came within six miles, he'd dive the boat and then resurface to continue the run. He'd yo-yo all the way to an attack position, if he had to.

"You made the right call," Rusty said.

"I made the call," Charlie partially agreed. Whether he'd made the right one or not remained an open question. It still galled him he'd halted the attack. He'd been surprised to discover how badly he'd wanted a win. Then there were the other repercussions. Would Cooper or even his own crew think he'd lost his nerve?

"I'm serious." Rusty frowned. "You…"

Charlie shot him a glance. "I, what?"

"You've done a lot of impressive things, brother, but that may have impressed me most."

"A lot of effort for no results impresses you? I'm not following your logic."

Rusty raised his binoculars to study the approaching storm. "Captains react to the pressure differently. Many end up too cautious. I was worried you might be the opposite."

"I wanted to shoot. I almost did."

"Robert E. Lee once said, 'I cannot trust a man to control others who cannot control himself.' Not a lot of men are able to exercise good judgment when they're facing the thing they want more than anything else."

"It isn't about what I want," Charlie said. "The overall result comes first. And I have to think about the lives of every man aboard."

"The bottom line is you have to pick your battles. Pick your battles then win the ones that matter most."

His friend sounded like Captain J.R. Kane. Charlie remembered his old commander saying, *That could be a good move. But there might be a better one.*

Not surprising to hear it from Rusty, who'd also mentored under Kane.

It rang true to him. All this time, Charlie had compared himself to Moreau, when he'd always agreed more with Kane's approach.

Make your strategy bold and your tactics cautious.

"You know, you'd make a great captain yourself," he said.

Rusty laughed. "Are you kidding? It's the easiest thing to be a critic. I second-guessed you during the attack, and that's on me."

"I'll always hear you out," Charlie told him. He thought about it some more and added, "In the right time and place."

The exec sighed. "Give me a good captain, but never make me one. That's my motto. I'd end up the overly cautious type. You put the overall results first, as it should be. I'd put the men first, not to mention my own neck. It reminds me of something else Robert E. Lee once said."

"What's that?"

"'To be a good soldier, you must love the army. To be a good commander, you must be willing to order the death of the thing you love.'"

A strong wind blew from the east. The seas became increasingly agitated. Storms traveled east to west in the tropics. Winds formed by equalizing pressure differences in the atmosphere flowed toward the equator, called the trade winds. These winds deflected to follow the earth's east-to-west rotation.

A westerly wind in the trades usually meant a tropical storm, but Charlie didn't need the wind or a barometer to tell him what was coming. He saw it. A massive dark wall of misty squalls, periodically whited out by intense flashes of light. He already felt a change in the air, which cooled but thickened. Thunder stomped and growled in the ether.

He lowered his binoculars. "We aren't going to make it."

The wind intensified until it howled around them, stirring up waves that swept over the main deck. Charlie dismissed the extra lookouts and had oilskins sent up. They were delivered just before the blackening sky lashed them with rain.

The storm arrived like a freight train.

CHAPTER FIFTEEN

TEMPEST

The *Sandtiger* rolled as the storm stirred up ten-foot swells that crashed into the struggling boat and washed her decks. The world dimmed to virtual night with near-zero visibility.

"Lookouts below!" Charlie ordered.

The men struggled down the shears and squeezed into the two-foot-wide hatch, shimmying down the ladder one by one.

"All engines on propulsion!"

A moment later, St. Elmo's fire flared at the tops of the shears. The men remaining on watch eyed the blue, luminous plasma.

"Wow," Rusty said.

Sailors once considered St. Elmo's fire a good omen. Charlie doubted it meant good luck for him. Even with all four mains driving the propellers, the colossal force of the raging seas was grinding down the *Sandtiger*'s speed.

A roller surged over the bridge and drained

away. The *Sandtiger* steered into the waves and found herself riding a swell as big as a hill. Charlie's stomach lurched as the *Sandtiger* crested, wobbled, and then slid into the trough. He slammed against the coaming, earning a fresh bruise.

"This ain't a storm," Hooker cried. "It's a god-damn typhoon!"

The sea lit up in a flash, followed seconds later by a terrific salvo of thunder. The rain thickened to sheets, drumming the deck.

"Recommend diving," Rusty shouted over the gale.

"We're staying on the surface as long as we can," Charlie shouted back. "We're losing bearing! We need to make as much way as possible!"

The *Sandtiger* lurched up an even taller crest and plunged into the trough, water smashing into the bridge. The men emerged from the waist-high flood, sputtering and staggering as their boat pitched and yawed.

"We're barely making thirteen knots now," Rusty said.

"We need to get as close as we can to the target, or we'll lose him for good!"

The wind roared and blasted them with incredible force.

"Conn, Bridge," he shouted into the gale. "Give me a sweep on the PPI!"

"Wait one, Bridge," Nixon said. "Captain, Chief Braddock recommends we dive. We're taking in too much water through the main induction."

"What do you think, Nix?"

"I agree with the chief. We're getting too many electrical grounds."

The boat needed the main induction to suck air used by the engines for propulsion and to charge the batteries. With multiple electrical grounds, he'd pay an escalating price for staying on the surface.

"Captain, Sugar Jig reports no contacts on the PPI," Nixon added. "The radar is barely making 5,000 yards."

"Very well," Charlie said, thinking hard.

Rusty flinched as another wall of water slammed across the bridge. "We've been at this over an hour, and we aren't making way, Skipper. We need to give it up."

Charlie bristled. He didn't give up. If he was the type who gave up, the *Yosai* would still be fighting, the Meteor would have killed a lot of Americans on Saipan, and he and his crew would be dead.

Stay on the bastard until he's on the bottom. Mush Morton's motto and one all the captains of the Silent Service had adopted as their own.

His stomach lurched as the *Sandtiger* crested another wave, this one tall as a mountain.

"Listen," Rusty said. "Even if we somehow caught up to the target, we couldn't attack!"

His friend was right. The high waves would wreak havoc on his torpedoes' accuracy, and he had no fish to waste on long odds.

Charlie cast one last longing gaze to the north, where the enemy steamed, out of sight. Vanishing along with his hopes of sinking the *Mamiya*.

He'd tried, but he was no longer doing any good staying on the surface.

He grit his teeth. "Very well. Clear the topsides! Conn, rig to dive!"

The main induction banged shut. Hooker raised the main hatch. He'd timed it after the last wave drained off the bridge. Still, seawater gushed all the way to the control room to splash the men and equipment there, evoking a round of curses.

Charlie slid to the deck and jumped aside as Rusty thudded after him.

The water pouring from above stopped.

"Hatch secured!" Hooker called down.

Soaked, bruised, and exhausted by his battering on the bridge, Charlie pulled off his oilskins. The diving alarm bonged.

Nixon said, "Pressure in the boat, green board, Captain. All compartments rigged to—"

Charlie staggered as the *Sandtiger* corkscrewed, pitching and rolling at the same time.

Men shouted in alarm as the boat went into a partial spin.

Nixon stumbled toward a bucket and vomited.

Charlie said, "Planes, take us—"

The boat rolled again and this time didn't stop.

The *Sandtiger* listed heavily, sending men and loose equipment sliding and crashing across the deck.

Charlie grabbed a section of overhead piping just in time, yelping as his feet dangled in air. He glanced across the compartment at the inclinometer, which showed the boat's list climbing from forty to fifty to sixty degrees.

She was going to capsize.

Then men and their boat groaned together as she righted herself.

Charlie's feet met the deck. "Planes, 200 feet! Take her down!"

No point in diving to periscope depth. Rain would curtain the periscope's glass. The rough waters would make good depth control almost impossible, resulting in frequent dunking of the scope.

The storm had effectively postponed the war in this stretch of the Pacific.

Down in the control room, the planesmen turned their big brass wheels in opposite directions. Bow planes rigged to dive, stern planes angling the submarine.

"Control, open all main vents," Rusty gasped.

The hydraulic manifoldman opened the vents to flood the ballast tanks with seawater, draining the boat's buoyancy.

The *Sandtiger* slid into the sea. She clawed for depth. The rolling ebbed until it was hardly noticeable.

Rusty picked himself up off the deck. "God. That was close."

Charlie understood this was his opportunity to say something bold or humorous. A story the crew would pass around. *Did you hear what the Old Man said? The guy's got balls!*

He felt too beaten up to fake it right now. "You all right, Nix?"

The engineering officer nodded, his face shifting from pale green to bright red. The list had tossed his vomit back onto his shirt. "Aye, Captain."

"Go get yourself cleaned up, and then report back to finish your watch."

"I'm hurt, Captain," Hooker said. "Think I broke a rib up on the bridge."

"You're relieved, Hook. Go see Doc on the double."

"Aye. Sorry, Captain."

"Percy, are you able to take the conn until Nixon returns?"

The officer blew out a ragged sigh and finally let go of the plotting table to which he'd been clinging for dear life. "Yup. I'm good."

"Mr. Percy has the deck and the conn," Charlie announced. "Get us onto a bearing of double-oh-five and keep us on it. The storm is slowing the enemy down too."

He wrote his orders in the Captain's Night Order Book. "Periscope checks every hour. As soon as the storm breaks, I want us surfaced and back on the hunt."

Percy nodded in a daze. His Aloha shirt had torn and was missing a button. "Aye, Captain."

"And find a replacement for Hook. I'll be in my bunk."

There, he'd sleep with the emergency call bell mounted over his head, which would ring if the boat was able to surface or otherwise ran into trouble.

Not that he honestly believed he could sleep right now.

Not with the storm preventing him from surfacing, which was already triggering his cleithrophobia.

And certainly not after today. So much effort with nothing to show for it.

CHAPTER SIXTEEN

WAITING

As expected, sleep eluded as him. Stretched out in his skivvies on his bunk, Charlie went over the attack again and again, wondering where he went wrong.

The problem was, if he had to do it all over again, he'd make the same decisions. He regretted only the lack of results.

That bothered him more than anything. He wanted to believe he had more control than he did over the outcome of a battle.

Stay on the bastard until he's on the bottom. A motto presenting a stark absolute that wasn't always possible in war. Mottos didn't account for typhoons.

Every passing hour carried his prey farther from him, along with his hopes of catching them. A storm like this could last eight hours or longer.

As Charlie finally began to drift into slumber, he sensed the walls closing in. The sweltering room became suffocating. Drenched in sweat, he rolled onto his side and clenched his eyes shut, willing himself to sleep.

No use. He rose and clicked on his desk lamp. Might as well do something productive. Pulling his logbook in front of him, he started writing.

A knock on the doorframe of his stateroom. He rubbed his aching eyes. "Come in."

Braddock parted the curtain. "Saw your light on and figured maybe you could use one of these, sir."

Charlie smiled. "Thanks, Chief. I could use a cup of joe."

The machinist held up a bag and grinned. "Beer."

"Beer's for winners, remember?"

"We're alive, ain't we? I know you didn't get to kill anything, but I count that as a win for today."

"All right," Charlie said. "Give me one. Grab a chair. We can talk about the air conditioning."

The chief settled his big frame on the edge of the bunk, pulled out two steel cans of Busch, and handed one over. "The AC is broke dick."

"I know it's broke dick. Can you fix it or not?"

Braddock cracked his beer open and drank from it. "Already did. Twice. We're lucky we're getting out of it what we're getting."

Charlie took his own swig. The fizz worked

its way down his gullet. Warm but just what he needed. "All right."

"Not a miracle worker," the chief muttered.

"I know how much you hate compliments, but you've taken the job by the horns. You're doing even better than I expected, and I expected a lot."

The sailor was a changed man in every respect. Even now, it made Charlie worry the old Braddock might show up again.

"I'm the same guy I was before," Braddock said. "My job changed, not me. It's a whole different ballgame when it ain't just your ass you got to worry about. Know what I mean?"

Charlie smiled. "I think I do."

"They're asshole knuckle draggers, but they're my knuckle draggers. I want to see them all get home."

"What about you? What comes after?"

"After the war? There's that optimism again."

"You must have some ideas."

"Sure do, sir." The sailor took another long pull and sighed. "I'm gonna screw everything in sight."

The obligatory answer for a sailor. "Duly noted. And after that?"

"Go somewhere else and screw everything there."

"You've got ambition," Charlie deadpanned.

"I don't know, sir. You spend a lot of time thinking about what comes after? Start hoping for it? Thinking you'll come back the same man you left? Believing you'll get home in one piece?"

Charlie contemplated his beer can. "I guess not."

"Three fucking years. Millions dead, and I got to kill my fair share. For what?"

"We all have our reasons for fighting."

"All right, I'll play. I guess I'll find a broad who can put up with me and start making babies. Get an honest job. Work hard to make some rich assholes even richer until I croak." He belched. "The American Dream. What about you?"

"Figure myself out before I make any decisions."

Braddock nodded sagely. "Of course. Guys like you are always looking at their belly buttons. I guess that's what makes you a good CO. In the engine rooms, it's a lot simpler. Everything is cause and effect."

"The jury's still out on whether I'll be a good captain."

"You were forced to take the conn from Hunter, Moreau, and Saunders. You did fine. Better than fine. If you didn't, you wouldn't be captain now."

Charlie finished his beer to hide his smile. The man had made a simple point, and it was true. Cause and effect. "Thanks for the confidence, Chief."

The big sailor scowled at the sudden intimacy. "I was just—ah, to hell with you, sir. I don't know why I bothered."

Braddock stomped from the room with the rest of the beer. Charlie waited until he was out of earshot before he laughed.

The man was full of surprises.

He set down his can and pulled on his service khakis. Sleep was an impossibility now. He'd just have to tough it out as he'd done before many times. The boat pushed and pulled around him. Nixon was shortening the depth as ordered to test the weather, which was still heavy.

He found Rusty tuning his fiddle in the wardroom. "Couldn't sleep?"

"Every time I closed my eyes, I saw a wall of water coming at me," the exec said. "Tonight would have been a good one to go into reversa."

Reversa, flipping the crew's schedule between day and night, during patrols when most action would occur after dark. Charlie already had his veterans on duty at night, and he made sure he'd be awakened during any confirmed nocturnal target sightings.

He shuffled to the tiny galley to pour himself a mug. "We'll try again tomorrow."

"We lost them," Rusty said. "They're gone."

"Looks that way." Charlie sighed as he returned to the room and sat at the table. "Hopefully, our contact report to Pearl will come back as a Fox to another submarine in the Philippines net."

The exec grinned. "You okay with another captain getting the glory?"

"We had our shot. As long as the *Mamiya* ends up on the bottom, I'll be happy."

And as long as I get to sink something else later, he thought.

"Nothing to do but wait, then."

Charlie gestured to Rusty's fiddle. "Play something. Maybe some of that mountain music you like. I'll join in."

His friend smiled. "'There'll Be Some Changes Made' it is."

Whenever Percy wasn't around to force some Gene Autry on them, Rusty liked to play a mix of old time and Appalachian music. Often, he ended up playing in thirds and fifths to produce a certain sound, slurred his long strokes to produce rapid noting, and didn't use the instrument's chin or shoulder rest.

It took everything Charlie had, at his skill level, to keep up. He tripped, recovered, and tripped again. Still, this song was one of his favorites, fast and jaunty. True to his nature, he gave it everything he had.

CHAPTER SEVENTEEN

OUT OF THE FRYING PAN

One song flowed into the next, melody and harmony. The next two hours flew past until Waldron arrived and served breakfast. Percy and Nixon showed up to pour themselves coffee from the galley and join Charlie and Rusty at the table.

Percy stared at his captain, who put his harmonica away and tucked into his eggs. "Did you play 'In the Jailhouse Now' without me?"

"Hillbilly music," Charlie told him, cheeks bulging.

"That's okay then, I guess."

The deck tilted as the *Sandtiger* planed up to periscope depth. Morrison was checking the weather's temper. Charlie froze, fork poised in front of his face. The boat rolled only slightly. He shot a glance at the 7MC mounted on the wall.

Moments later, the conning tower called.

He picked up the phone. "This is the captain."

"The storm's passing, sir," Morrison reported.

"Any contacts?"

"Nothing, Captain."

"Take another look then surface the boat if practical," Charlie said. "The exec and I will be there in a minute."

"It's after sunrise," Rusty said in alarm.

"We need to replenish our air and batteries. See if we can make some way north. We'll get a radar sweep in while we're at it."

Rusty nodded. He didn't like it, but there was no other way to get the boat fresh air and power.

"All compartments, rig to surface," the 1MC blared.

They mounted to the conning tower as Morrison ordered all compartments to shut the bulkhead flappers.

"All compartments report rigged to surface," the telephone talker said.

Morrison came to attention at the sight of the captain. "Ready to surface in every respect, Captain."

"Very well. Take her up."

The helmsman pulled the handle to blast the surfacing alarm.

Morrison smiled at the commotion, clearly enjoying himself. "Control, blow all main ballast!"

High-pressure air blasted into the ballast tanks, displacing the water and buoying the boat. The planesmen angled the *Sandtiger* for the ascent.

Morrison: "Lookouts, report to the tower!"

The quartermaster and three sailors reported for the watch as the *Sandtiger* burst from the sea.

Charlie checked the dead reckoning indicator, which gave him the boat's latitude and longitude, then studied the plot. He was too close to the shore. "Helm, come right to oh-four-five. Radar, warm up the Sugar Jig and stand by. Sugar Dog, give me a sweep for planes as soon as you're able."

Starting over. He hadn't gained anything, but he hadn't lost anything either. Today was a clean slate.

The foul air whistled through the open hatch as the boat vented the pressure that had built up during the night. The quartermaster called out the all clear. Charlie and Rusty followed the lookouts onto the bridge.

The morning air, already warm and sticky, stank. Dead jellyfish lay strewn across the decks, deposited by the rough seas and as good as glued.

Charlie ignored it and scanned the surroundings with his binoculars, grateful to be out of the boat's noxious atmosphere and back in the open air. The seas had calmed. A mild wind blew from the northeast. Despite a few scattered rainsqualls, the horizon was clear all around, the sky partially obscured with cloud cover. Nothing was happening on Samar. No patrol planes, though that would change soon enough. And no ships in sight.

The *Sandtiger* crossed a light chop, heading toward the open sea. The conn passed on the message from the SD radarman. No plane contacts.

He said into the bridge phone, "Sugar Jig, give me that sweep on the PPI."

Overhead, the radar swiveled on its mast, sweeping the surface of the sea.

"Back to square one," Rusty said.

Charlie surveyed the empty sea. "Looks that way. Ideas?"

"You're onto something by staying close to the coast. We could work our way up to Luzon and then back down to Hernani. Something will turn up."

"Something," Charlie agreed. "I'd like to peek into Borongan next. Maybe we'll find some coasters."

At this point, anything would do.

The bridge speaker blared: "Multiple contacts! Bearing, three-five-oh, oh-one-oh off the starboard bow, range 25,000 miles."

Charlie and Rusty exchanged surprised grins. A convoy, heading their way?

"How many contacts?" Charlie asked.

"Wait, one ... One hundred and five, Captain."

"Repeat that, conn."

"One-oh-five. We counted twice."

After a few seconds processing this news, Charlie said, "Very well."

"Make that one hundred and ten, Captain. More keep popping up."

"Over a hundred ships," Rusty said. "Jesus. Something big is happening. What do you think? Ours or theirs?"

Charlie aimed his binoculars east. "We'll find out soon enough."

After some waiting, the first ships appeared along the horizon. They were destroyers, and plenty of them.

"They're American," he said, setting off a cheer from the lookouts.

More vessels popped along the horizon, creating a solid wall of ships. Destroyers, battleships, cruisers, and fleet carriers.

Rusty laughed. "That's Halsey's Third Fleet. It's happening."

"What's that?"

"I'm guessing, but I think we might be invading the Philippines."

Charlie chuckled. "Perkins, start flashing recognition signals."

"Aye, Captain," the quartermaster of the watch said.

God, it was beautiful. He was looking at a vast fleet. America's clenched fist reached across the world to smite the empire that had attacked it.

"We take the Philippines, we'll have bombers that much closer to Tokyo," Rusty said.

"We'll isolate Japan from the rest of Asia."

"And we can start invading the home islands."

"Then we take Tokyo."

"Then it's over." Rusty guffawed. "It'll finally be over. God!"

"And we can go home," Charlie said.

The exec raised his fist. "Come on, you beautiful sons of bitches!"

"Plane, approaching!" one of the lookouts cried.

Charlie spotted it. A bomber had swooped from the cloud cover and was howling toward the *Sandtiger*.

"That's not a Betty," Perkins said, referring to a Japanese patrol bomber. He flashed recognition signals at it. "It's one of ours."

Charlie wasn't about to take any chances, remembering the Navy fighter that strafed the *Sandtiger* in the Battle of the Philippine Sea.

The plane continued to scream toward the submarine with a zero angle on the bow.

He punched the bridge diving alarm. "Clear the topsides! Take her down, emergency! Dive, dive, dive!"

The men tumbled down the ladder, the submarine already angling into the sea. Past the shears, the Navy torpedo bomber shrieked at them in a glide bombing run. A TBF-1 Avenger manufactured by Grumman and General Motors, swooping down on its fifty-four-foot wingspan like a giant bird of prey.

In the Battle of the Atlantic, these planes were notorious U-boat killers.

Charlie secured the hatch as the *Sandtiger* submerged and clawed for depth. He reached the conning tower.

"Thirty feet!" Rusty called out.

Charlie grabbed the nearest handhold. "Rig for depth charge—"

The Avenger's bomb splashed into the water and exploded close astern.

CHAPTER EIGHTEEN

BROACHED

The shockwave struck the *Sandtiger* like a giant hammer.

Light flared in Charlie's eyes. The submarine around him was disintegrating, shards breaking off and flying up and disappearing into a pure white sky.

Then he was back in the conning tower. The deck tilted as the stern rose, the superstructure still trembling.

Charlie gasped, horrified by his awful vision.

His hearing returned next, a clamor of men screaming at each other.

The boat was *rising*.

"Our stern broached!" Rusty shouted at him.

Charlie gaped at the overhead bulkhead. Right now, the *Sandtiger*'s ass was sticking above the water.

While the Avenger circled for another bombing run.

Horror hardened into rage. An American was trying to kill him. An excited pilot with limited awareness who'd spotted a ship surfaced near islands targeted for invasion. The pilot thought he was doing the right thing. Thought he was a hero for doing it.

But Charlie was angry with himself most of all for not diving the boat the instant he spotted Third Fleet. He should have known they'd be in the kind of jumpy mood where they shot first and asked questions later.

Helpless, the *Sandtiger* struggled at a steep down angle.

Then, with a sickening flop of gravity, she plunged nose first toward the seafloor. A relief, though he now faced a different kind of danger.

The boat was out of control.

"Hard rise on the planes!" Charlie ordered. "Blow bow buoyancy!"

"Passing seventy-five feet!" Rusty called out.

"Blow safety!"

Chief of the Boat Spike Sullivan called up from the control room: "Planes are stuck on dive, sir!"

"Blow all ballast!"

"Passing 150 feet!"

"Chief, get control of the planes!"

"We're on it, sir!"

Below, several sailors joined the planesman

and grabbed hold of the wheel. Roaring with the strain, they began to wrestle the jammed planes to hard rise.

"Passing 250 feet!"

"Come on!" Charlie growled.

"It's moving, Captain!" Spike said.

He was right. After a nosedive straight to 320 feet, the *Sandtiger* began to level off.

"We're slowing," Rusty said. "We're getting buoyancy."

Another sickening change of gravity.

The boat began to lurch back toward the surface.

"Get us under control, Chief!" Charlie said.

Morrison leaned to the open hatch and yelled into the control room, "Vent the tanks!"

"One of the tanks isn't venting!" Spike yelled back.

"Do it manually," Charlie ordered. "Now, Chief!"

"Already on it, sir!"

Rusty: "One hundred feet!"

Charlie gazed up again at the bulkhead in horror. In moments, they'd be back under the Avenger's crosshairs.

"We're broaching again," Rusty said. "We're surfacing!"

The *Sandtiger* broke the water.

The air pressure in the conning tower suddenly jumped, which meant the last tank was venting.

Achieving negative buoyancy at last, the submarine plummeted into another dive.

This time at a gentler incline. Which was good because they were less likely to lose control again, but bad because they weren't making depth fast enough.

"Fifty-five feet—"

Splash!

Charlie flinched and waited for it.

The second five-hundred-pound bomb exploded off the port beam, a muffled boom that struck the boat with an air-rending bang and buckled the hull in and out. The jolt hurled sailors sprawling to the rolling deck, shook metal seams and fastenings loose, blew a cloud of paint chips off the bulkheads. Dials and gauges danced crazily and popped. The light bulbs rattled and shattered, plunging the compartment into darkness. A high-pressure line ruptured, whistling compressed air.

The section of piping Charlie was using as a handhold wrenched loose, gushing water. He tumbled to the deck, which had buckled and still trembled in a series of aftershocks.

Like being on the ground floor of a collapsing building.

Men moaned and coughed on air thick with cork insulation dust. The superstructure vibrated like a tuning fork, filling the fouled atmosphere with a deep, menacing hum that burrowed into their ears.

By now, the emergency lighting, supplied by the battery, should have switched on, but the bulbs were broken. They were in the dark. The overload relay breakers had popped. The *Sandtiger* drifted in the water without power.

Charlie heaved himself onto hands and knees. "We need light."

A hand lantern flared to life. "It's me. Morrison. I got it."

Rusty finished a coughing fit and spat. "I don't know whether to kill that pilot or give him a medal. He's good."

Charlie had to agree. Hard as it was to fight the Japanese, he'd far rather fight them than the Americans at this point in the war.

Right now, apparently, he had no choice in the matter.

The battle lantern's light glared across the conning tower, revealing pale gasping faces, warped pipes, ruptured valves, burst gauges. The soundman attacked a spraying valve with a wrench. Cork dust and water sparkled in the swinging light beam. Compressed air howled from the ruptured high-pressure line.

"Our own side!" somebody was raving down in the control room. "I'm gonna kill that son of a bitch!"

"Injuries?" Charlie said. "Anybody injured?"

Barkley, the SD radarman, said he thought his wrist was broken. Everybody else had cuts and bruises but was otherwise fit for duty.

Two surviving light bulbs flared to life.

"We've got power," Rusty said.

God bless the A-gangers. The electrician's mates had acted quickly to pop fresh fuses into the electrical panel.

"Very well," Charlie said. "I need damage reports. Exec, get us back into good trim. Morrison, get the A-gang up here to start repairs, and get this water pumped out. Barkley, go see Doc."

The compressed air's whistle died as the auxiliarymen closed off that section of piping. An A-ganger mounted to the conning tower and installed fresh light bulbs.

"Light screws, bearing two-nine-oh," the soundman said.

Charlie and Rusty exchanged a nervous glance. Third Fleet wasn't happy just bombing them. Now they were sending a destroyer to finish the job.

"He's echo ranging," the soundman added.

"Helm, come right to three-four-oh," Charlie said. "All ahead full."

The helmsman repeated the order and turned the boat.

"Have Mr. Nixon report to the control room and find me a thermocline," Charlie added, relieved the *Sandtiger* still had propulsion and steering. "And somebody tell that skipper, if my boat gets even so much as a scratch, I'm going to kick his ass."

"You take the skipper, Captain," the SJ radarman said. "I'll handle the pilot."

The sailors cracked grins.

Sometimes, you had to put on a front for the men. It wasn't about him, about faking it to put on a show. It was about his crew's morale. Right now, they needed to see their captain as a rock.

He was going to have to be to get them out of this alive.

CHAPTER NINETEEN

HUNTED

Sound: "Target still approaching on two-nine-oh bearing, range 5,000 yards."

"Very well," Charlie said. "Helm, come right to double-oh-five."

"Come right to double-oh-five, aye, Captain."

Soon, they'd be far from shore and reaching for the open expanses of the Philippine Sea. Plenty of thermoclines to hide under out there.

"Splashes!"

Thunder rolled in the deep. Depth charges. The blast waves nudged the *Sandtiger*'s stern.

The bomber had marked its final sighting of the submarine with smoke. The destroyer had zeroed in on the spot and dumped a series of charges.

Charlie frowned. Something about the sounds of the attack wasn't right, but he couldn't put his finger on it.

"He's got throwers," the soundman hissed from his station.

That was it. The explosions sounded too far from the propellers to be depth charges dumped from the stern. The destroyer had K-guns, which launched depth charges up to 150 yards. The explosives bracketed a submarine above and below, creating a tremendous shockwave that could smash a submersible.

Which meant Charlie wasn't facing a destroyer up there. No, it was a destroyer escort, a light-weight tin can. Probably a *Buckley* class, with a crew of 186. While escorts had only three-inch guns and fewer torpedo tubes, they carried an impressive anti-submarine arsenal. In fact, their sole purpose was to destroy submarines.

Great.

"He crossed our track and is coming right astern," the soundman reported.

"Control, check for fuel leaks," Charlie said. "We might be giving away our position."

If the bombs had caused a leak, oil floating to the surface would reveal a clear path to the *Sandtiger*.

The telephone talker received another damage report. "Chief Braddock says the bombs blew out the forward engine room gasket, and the hatch is leaking water."

"Tell him to do the best he can to stop the leak until we can surface."

"Aye, Captain."

Of all the damage reports that flooded in during the bombing attack's aftermath, this was the most serious. Water was gushing into the boat through the forward engine room hatch, which would make her heavy, slower, less maneuverable. Little could be done about it for now.

Diving deep was riskier because of the increased pressure. The water had to be pumped out, meaning he couldn't go to silent running until it was absolutely necessary.

The sound of the destroyer escort's screws grew louder until it filled the conning tower and resonated through the hull. As it closed, it switched to short-scale echo ranging, filling the boat with the squeal of its rapid pings.

A series of thuds above.

"Splashes off the port bow!"

Charlie tensed for the shock. Nothing. Then he yelled, "Helm, all stop!"

The *Sandtiger* coasted on her momentum.

"What's going on?" Rusty wondered.

"Hedgehog," Charlie told him.

The deadliest anti-submarine weapon in the war.

British-designed, the twenty-four-barrel mortar fired shells similar to potato mashers. While depth charges exploded at a set depth, these bombs detonated only when they struck a hard surface. Namely, the hull of a submarine.

Charlie suppressed a shudder. "Control, do we have a thermocline?"

"No, Captain," Spike said from the control room.

"Very well. Helm, come left to three-five-oh. All ahead full."

"We're heading back to Samar," Rusty said. "Into shallow waters."

"That's right."

The *Sandtiger* wasn't leaking oil. She was heading away from the approaching escort and toward open sea. The best escape route but also predictable.

The destroyer escort had known exactly where she was going.

"Two sets of light screws," the soundman said. "Bearing two-eight-oh, one-one-oh relative. They're echo ranging."

"Well played," Charlie muttered.

The three ships had him boxed in nicely, forcing him to go in the direction he'd already chosen himself, back toward Samar.

"Helm, come right to triple-oh."

The screws and pinging intensified as the tin cans closed in. Charlie glared up at the bulkhead, his rage returning.

His boat was getting heavier by the minute, and he couldn't go deep. Three destroyers were closing in, one of them specially designed as a sub killer.

His own country seemed dead set on killing him.

The only way out was to outsmart them. But how?

Whoosh whoosh whoosh whoosh

PING-PING

Rusty paled. "He's got a fix on us."

The destroyer escort darted right, pacing the *Sandtiger* to starboard. Thuds overhead as the ship fired its side-throwers.

"Helm, all back, emergency!" Charlie cried.

"Splashes!"

"All stop! Sound, tell me which way he goes next—"

The depth charges tumbled into the water in a bracket pattern ahead.

WHAM! WHAM! WHAM!

The shockwaves struck the bow and rattled the *Sandtiger* and her crew like a jar of peanuts.

"Helm, steer double-oh-five," Charlie said. "Sound, call out the target's bearings. Helm, as sound feeds you the bearings, take the steering."

"Captain?"

"I want you to steer us onto the target's course and stay in his wake. Stay on him like glue. Understand?"

The helmsman nodded. "Aye, aye, Captain."

Rusty said, "That'll buy us some time."

"We could try Morse code, Captain," Morrison said.

"Explain that."

"Go to silent running and wait until two of the DEs get close enough. Rise to periscope depth and bang out a message on a pipe. 'We're Americans,' something like that. Then surface. They won't shoot if we're right between them."

"It's not a terrible idea," Rusty said.

Charlie shook his head. "It's too risky. We know there's one crazy pilot up there. They might have called in more planes. I'd consider it our Hail Mary."

"Then what's the plan, Skipper? We can't stay on his stern forever. It won't take long for that tin can to get wise."

"We're going to have to test our new countermeasures. Morrison, stand by to fire evasion devices. All compartments, stand by for silent running."

"The bubbler or the sonar decoy?" Morrison asked.

"The sonar decoy. We'll fire six from the bow tubes. Three-second intervals."

The torpedo officer's idea had been too risky, but something else was driving Charlie's decision-making. A bit of pride. A desire to beat the American skipper at his own game. A part of him still couldn't believe an American was trying to kill him and his crew. He wasn't having it.

The forward torpedo doors thudded open.

"He's speeding up, Captain," the soundman said.

"Now or never," Rusty said. "He's trying to shake us."

The game was up.

"Forward Torpedo reports sonar decoys loaded and ready to fire, Captain," Morrison said. "Shoot anytime."

"Very well. Fire all decoys!"

"Firing all decoys! Decoys away."

"Helm, all stop!" Charlie ordered. "Right full rudder! All ahead one-third."

The helmsman turned the rudder hard over, swinging the boat to starboard.

"Rig for silent running."

Throughout the submarine, the crew secured and dogged the watertight doors between compartments, shut down ventilation blowers and refrigerator motors, and put the helm and planes on manual operation. The air conditioning gasped to a halt.

The telephone talker said, "All compartments report rigged for silent running. Sonar decoys are running straight and normal."

Charlie's response came out a stage whisper. "Very well."

Now he'd see how good the countermeasures were. In the meantime, there was nothing to do but wait. The ten sailors packed into the conning tower sweated as the temperature immediately climbed even higher.

WHAM! WHAM! WHAM!

The sailors grinned at their stations. The depth charges were exploding off the port quarter. The escort had taken the bait and was pounding the sonar beacons.

Charlie leaned toward the helmsman. "Come to oh-eight-oh."

Another round of depth charges banged in the waters astern.

The *Sandtiger* glided silently between the other two destroyers until she reached the open sea.

CHAPTER TWENTY

LICKING WOUNDS

Cruising at periscope depth north of Third Fleet, the *Sandtiger* secured from battle stations and silent running. Battered and waterlogged, her bow slightly raised, she struggled to maintain speed.

Nonetheless, Charlie planned to take her into action by nightfall.

Standing in the forward engine room's foot-deep, oily, brackish water, Braddock swept his arms across the pulsing machinery. "The water's coming in faster than we can pump it out, sir. We can't repair it until we surface."

Behind him, seawater cascaded from a ruptured gasket, the hatch warped by the force of the bomb's detonation. A line of sailors had formed a bucket brigade leading to Aft Torpedo. They bailed hard to keep the water level from reaching the propulsion motors and reduction gears. Many of them wore their skivvy shirts tied around their necks and heads to soak up their perspiration. The foul air had grown so humid that sweat didn't dry, and condensation streamed down the bulkheads.

Charlie scratched his itchy stubble. "If we surface, we might have to go through all that again, so give it to me straight."

The chief thought about it. "You got one hour, sir."

Charlie glanced at Nixon for his opinion.

"It depends," the engineering officer said then launched into a detailed description of the variables involved.

Charlie waited until he came up for air then said, "So an hour?"

Nixon thought about it some more, then said, "That should work."

"Great," growled Braddock, who lacked his captain's patience. "We got other problems too. The number four engine was wrenched right off its mount. The port engine compressor is damaged. The starboard main motor bearing is running so hot it's smoking and has to be constantly oiled—"

Charlie had already heard the chief go through the engine and motor rooms' litany of wounds. Braddock was showing off for his engine snipes by upstaging Nixon, who again seemed oblivious to their rivalry.

"Very well," he said at last. "What about the men, Chief? What's their temper?"

"Pissed off and itching to shoot something."

"I'm working on that."

"I figured you were. Me, I'd be happy if you could work out a brilliant plan where we don't get bombed again. That would be terrific." Putting aside his usual charm, Braddock raised his chin in pride. "You should know not a single man lost their shit. They did their jobs."

"Thank you, Chief. Carry on. We need all repairs completed by sundown."

Nixon tilted his head. "What happens at sundown?"

"I'm hoping we'll be doing some shooting."

The snipes stopped their work and stared, hoping to hear more. *Let them wonder*, Charlie decided.

The boat was in bad shape. He had little time to act, and he might not even find any targets where he wanted to go. Oh, and Third Fleet might try to sink him along the way. So no promises.

Still, he wanted the crew to know their captain was working on getting them into the kind of action where they could shoot back. He didn't feel self-conscious anymore about putting on a show. Right now, they needed to believe.

Braddock crossed his arms. "What happens at sundown is the captain expects a miracle to happen. You heard my list of—"

145

"You do your part, Chief, and I'll do mine," Charlie said. "Then we can break out that beer you stowed."

"You think beer will get all these repairs done in a matter of hours."

"I'm willing to bet on it."

The chief snorted and turned to his snipes. "All right, you knuckleheads. You heard the captain! We got a miracle to pull off."

"I'll stay here and pitch in, Captain," Nixon said.

"What about me? You need an extra hand, Chief?"

"You do your part, Captain, and I'll do mine. Mr. Nixon, on the other hand, I can use, as long as he follows our department's no-talking rule. The air conditioning needs fixing again."

"Very well," Charlie said. "Nix, come find me later. I've got a special job for you."

"Aye, Captain." Nixon rolled up his sleeves to work.

Charlie left them to it and checked in with the departments. He learned what he could about the repair work and got out of their hair as quickly as possible. This was when all the training really showed. The boat was in good hands.

The radio transmitter tubes were blown and had to be replaced so the *Sandtiger* could radio their situation to Pearl. After ensuring the radio would be operational, he exited the control room and headed to the wardroom for coffee. Along the way, he passed a cheerful Percy who was handing out shots of medicinal brandy. For the communications officer, getting bombed was almost worth it to splice the mainbrace and get his depth charge medicine.

In the wardroom, Rusty was slumped over the table sound asleep, a full mug of lukewarm coffee set before him. Large sweat stains blackened his chest and armpits. The exec stirred and rubbed his face as Charlie took a seat.

"Well," Rusty said. "That was something."

"It was good practice for the real thing."

He scoffed. "The practice nearly killed us. I'm glad those tin cans are on our side."

Charlie dropped the pretense. "Yeah, no kidding."

"Now that we've had our exercise, I imagine we'll go north and see what turns up."

Charlie sipped his coffee, which as always for him was strong and black. "South. We're going back to Hernani tonight."

The exec glanced around to ensure nobody was in earshot. "What the hell are you thinking?"

"If you're right about an invasion of the Philippines, Third Fleet is here to stay. By now, the Japs know the Navy is here, and any ship in port is going to get out of Dodge. They'll do it tonight."

"What do you expect to find?"

"We already know Hernani is being used as a pickup or refueling station. I don't expect to find any more big prizes, but we might get lucky and run into some coasters bolting for Manila. I need to give the men something to shoot at."

"Or we'll be taking a big risk getting there only to find nothing."

Charlie shrugged. "One thing I've learned, Rusty, is this game is a mix of chess and poker. Everything is risk. Risk and reward."

"Responsibility too. You aren't just betting chips, you know."

"Either way, if you want zero risk, you aren't in the game. If we find nothing at Hernani, we'll go north and try Borongan and every other port town this side of Samar."

"We've been out here over three weeks," the exec said. "It *would* be nice to shoot our fish at a target, or this Rusty is gonna get rusty."

Charlie took another swig from his mug. "I'm ready to start throwing rocks at sampans." He smirked. "So, do you still see me as good luck?"

"After seeing how you evaded those tin cans, brother, I'm glad you're on our side too."

He checked his watch. "Time to surface, or we might be swimming to Hernani. I want the boat in good trim and fighting shape by sundown."

Nixon toted a bucket of water into the wardroom and set it on the deck. Seawater, which he'd heat up later and use to wash his clothes. "AC is fixed, Captain. It should start feeling cooler in here soon."

"Good work," Charlie said.

"You missed your calling as an A-ganger, Nix," Rusty said.

"No, thanks. I like being an officer. But today, I'm going to be an auxiliaryman. I'm going to fix everything needing fixing." The engineering officer smiled. "Just to see the look on Chief Braddock's face."

Rusty chuckled. "I'd like to see that look myself."

So Nixon wasn't as oblivious to Braddock's attitude as Charlie had thought. He couldn't beat the chief in an asshole contest, so he'd show him up at his own game, which was fixing broke-dick equipment.

Charlie said, "How'd you like to really stick it to the engine rooms?"

Nixon's face lit up. "You said you had a special job for me."

"Remember that machine you rigged up in the control room that makes ice cream?"

"Captain Saunders made me get rid of it."

"I want you to rebuild it. If all goes well tonight, we'll be celebrating with beer courtesy of Mr. Percy and Chief Braddock."

"I don't like beer," said Nixon.

Rusty picked up on it. "They're celebrating. Then a few days later, here's the crew eating ice cream, courtesy of Mr. Nixon."

The engineering officer's face stretched into a rare grin. "It'll drive Braddock crazy."

CHAPTER TWENTY-ONE

RETURN

Braddock pulled off a miracle, aided in no small part by his competition with Nixon's mechanical genius and the promise of beer. At 1300, the *Sandtiger* surfaced to repair the leaks and expel the rest of the water in her pump room and bilges. By 1930, she'd radioed Pearl and completed a trim dive. By 2030, she was still heavy but on the move at last, cruising west by southwest on sixty percent power and ninety percent of the four engines' maximum speed.

On the bridge, legs braced against the boat's roll, Charlie drank in the pure, sweet air as he scanned the dark for ships, enemy or friendly. Both navies, it seemed, wanted to sink the *Sandtiger* right now. But the seas were empty. Third Fleet had disappeared as mysteriously as it had come.

Maybe Rusty was wrong, and they were headed to Taiwan instead.

He lowered his binoculars and studied his torpedo officer, who leaned against the bridge coaming with his own glasses pressed to his eyes. "How are you, Morrison?"

The man turned to him grinning. "Honestly? It's like a movie, but I'm in it."

Charlie smirked. "I remember that feeling well."

For as long as he could remember, submariners had given him advice, all of it ponderable, most of it useful, some of it life-saving. As captain, he was now expected to give some of his own, based on what he'd learned.

He added, "Then when things go really bad, you realize it isn't a movie. You aren't the star. You're just a man, and men die, often for no reason."

"Yes, sir," Morrison said soberly. "I won't go off half-cocked. I'll be careful."

Charlie sighed. The man had completely missed his point, but no matter. Words couldn't change the minds of young warriors. That craving to be tested, which Rusty had once so colorfully called a death wish. The only thing that cured it was the test itself. The horror of real combat. For Charlie, the turning point had been his midnight battle with the *Mizukaze*.

He decided to let Morrison have his dreams. The young man didn't need a jaded officer telling him what was what. Until he'd experienced it for himself, he couldn't understand it no matter how it was phrased.

"You do that," Charlie said. "You be careful. You clear on the plan?"

"My men are ready. They're chomping at the bit."

"Don't get your hopes too high. We may find only a few fishing boats."

"Your last hunch worked out."

"It wasn't a hunch. Captains don't have a sixth sense. It's just good submarining. The ability to read probabilities, to be exact."

"Whatever you call it, I trust it, Captain."

Charlie grimaced and went back to staring at the dark. The torpedo officer reminded Charlie of himself so strongly it was equal measures irritating and flattering. Right now, Morrison regarded him the way he had regarded Captain Kane. More of that responsibility Rusty was talking about.

And not just Morrison. Every one of his officers could command their own boats. It was his job to help them along, mentor them, cultivate their abilities.

"I could be wrong," he said.

"If you are, then we'll try again."

Charlie smiled. Good answer. "Do you play chess, Morrison?"

"Some, but I'm not too good at it."

"It's about time you got good. We'll play soon."

"Aye, sir. And what about you, sir?"

"What about me, Morrison?"

"How are you doing?"

Charlie remembered how Braddock put it. "Pissed off and wanting to shoot something."

"Bridge, Conn," the bridge speaker blatted.

"Go ahead, Conn."

"We're two miles from the harbor, still bearing two-six-oh."

"Very well."

The cloudy and moonless sky was ideal for his purposes. The black mass of Samar sprawled ahead. The *Sandtiger* followed roughly the same path into Matarinao Bay the *Mamiya* used to leave it.

The surrounding land was dark. Was there an alert coastal watcher out there, maybe on Anahap Island, peering back at him?

Unless Hernani was somehow hiding more destroyers, it didn't matter. Any ships anchored there would have to pass by him to get out.

"Conn, Bridge. Stand by to dive."

Charlie cleared the topsides and shimmied down to the conning tower. The diving alarm sounded as the *Sandtiger* plunged to periscope depth and changed course again, now heading north toward the small town nestled along the coast.

Percy called out soundings, which matched the charts. There wasn't much water under their keel, but they still had room to maneuver. Charlie reduced speed.

"Up scope." He crouched and rose with the periscope, sweeping Hernani and its docks. "Gentlemen, we are back in business."

"Twenty-three feet under the keel," Percy called out.

Shaving it close. "All stop."

Morrison eyed him hopefully. "Captain? What do you see?"

Charlie studied the targets. "I'm looking at a coaster, heavily camouflaged with tree branches, around 250 tons... A big two-mast schooner, probably used to carry rice, around 150 tons... A fifty-ton sea truck, wooden-hulled... And a gunboat, 250 tons. They're all loading. They're getting ready to leave. Down scope."

Morrison said, "Thank you, Captain."

None of the targets were worth a torpedo.

"Think you could take them with the deck gun and your commandos?"

"Just say the word, sir."

Charlie regarded his crew. "What about the rest of you? Ready for a fight?"

The grimy, bearded sailors roared at their stations, pissed off and ready to shoot.

"Battle stations," Charlie said. "Stand by to surface! Stand by for gun action!"

CHAPTER TWENTY-TWO

GIVE 'EM THE WORKS

The *Sandtiger* hovered at periscope depth just 500 yards from Hernani's docks. With the ballast tanks filled with enough air to surface, the planesmen strained at the wheels to keep the submarine submerged.

The five-inch-gun crew stood ready in the wardroom under the gun tower hatch while a supply party stacked shells from the magazine. Armed to the teeth, Morrison's commandos and the AA gun crews filled the conning tower ladder leading up to the main hatch. They wore red goggles to better adapt to night vision when they reached the topsides.

Beneath the hatch, Charlie waited with Hooker, who held a rubber mallet.

"Surface anytime, Skipper!" Rusty called up.

"Commence the attack," Charlie told him. "Give 'em the works, men!"

The grimy, bearded sailors howled a blood-thirsty cheer.

"Aye, aye, Captain," Rusty said. "Blow ballast! Surface! Gun action!"

The klaxon honked. Down in the control room, the air manifoldman blasted high-pressure air into the ballast tanks. The planesmen fought to keep the boat from surfacing, then let go and reversed the planes.

The *Sandtiger* shot straight up like an elevator and broke the surface on an even keel.

Hooker undogged the hatch and shoved it open. Morrison blew a whistle. The gun crews poured onto the deck to man the five-inch deck gun and AA cannons. Charlie climbed up and took in the scene. The gunboat, coaster, schooner, and sea truck, all anchored, some of the ships still loading.

He'd caught them with their pants down.

Morrison had drilled his crew until they could ready the five-inch gun in fifty seconds. While this gun, being the same carried by destroyers, struck with an awful punch, the AA cannons were similarly fierce against small targets. The *Sandtiger* had been modified in dry dock, the plating around her periscope shears removed, which produced good gun positions. The Navy had given her a forty-millimeter Bofors and a twin twenty-millimeter Oerlikon AA cannon.

Morrison cried: "FIRE!"

The gun boomed with a blinding flash and puff of smoke that washed into the bay. The round struck the dock next to the ironclad, hurling a cloud of dust and splinters in the air. The empty shell clanged from the breech. Japanese sailors screamed the alarm and scrambled to raise anchors.

They were sitting ducks, and they knew it.

The Bofors pounded and sent hot metal into the coaster's wheelhouse, and the Oerlikon chattered at the sea truck. Tracer rounds arced toward their targets. The AA guns kept them pinned until Morrison finished with the gunboat.

The deck gun banged again and again. The gunboat was burning, its bridge a tangle of metal scrap, without returning a single shot. Japanese sailors threw themselves into the water. Charlie almost felt bad for them, but after weeks of frustration, his blood sang at finally being in decisive combat.

"Shift fire to second target," he called. "Range, 500 yards!"

"Aye, aye!" Morrison answered.

They were shooting fish in a barrel here, but from the way the torpedo officer was fighting, you'd think he and his boys were taking down a flattop.

The gun pumped round after round into the

coaster. The ship slowly listed and sank in the mud, its camouflage ablaze.

The sea truck floundered while the large two-mast schooner was making sail, reaching from the dock under heavy AA gunfire.

"Contact!" Hooker cried, pointing.

An *Azio*-class minelayer, hidden behind the gunboat, had raised anchor and was coming on with a bone in its teeth.

"Right full rudder!" Charlie ordered. "Shift fire to the minelayer!"

The *Sandtiger* turned hard-a-starboard. Morrison grinned and bawled fresh orders, having the time of his life. Charlie blinked at the startling crack of Japanese explosive rounds, which raked the water off their beam. It wouldn't take them long to find the range.

"Rudder amidships! Steady on this course, all ahead full!"

The deck gun swiveled on its mount and boomed at the gunboat, striking the forecastle, which erupted in dust and spinning metal shards. The minelayer flashed with a heart-stopping bang as it brought its own deck gun into action. The shell tore the air overhead and splashed in the bay.

Morrison corrected aim and hurled shell after shell toward the enemy's gun, smashing the minelayer with terrific effect.

"God, he's good," Charlie said.

"Captain!" Hooker pointed at the schooner, which now lay on a convergent path with the *Sandtiger*.

"Steady on this course."

"Oh." The quartermaster grabbed hold of the coaming, bracing himself.

The *Sandtiger* rammed the schooner's bow, which splintered at the impact. The commandos sprayed the deck with small arms fire and threw grappling hooks like pirates of old. They clambered aboard with demolition charges, shooting anything that moved while Japanese sailors leaped into the water.

"Helm, all stop," Charlie ordered.

The *Azio*'s gun had fallen silent under Morrison's withering barrage. Charlie spared a glance and spotted one of his sailors being carried below. No time to find out who it was. The fighting, which was racing to its conclusion, demanded his full attention.

The minelayer had stopped dead in the water and drifted, helpless, as Morrison targeted it below the waterline. The gunboat floated unmanned on a burning oil slick, its bridge a smoking ruin. The coaster was sunk in the mud, and the sea truck's wooden hull had shattered under heavy fire, turning the small ship into a wreck. Garbage and debris bobbed on the water.

The commandos returned from the schooner. The *Sandtiger* backed away as the demolition charges blew out its hull below the waterline. The ship pitched and sank bow first into the bay.

On shore, the local garrison was finally getting into action. Machine gun fire winked in the darkness. Charlie kept the *Sandtiger* on station long enough for Morrison to pump another score of rounds into the gunboat, which refused to sink. At midnight, he called off the gun attack and showed the dying ship his stern, finishing it off with a single torpedo that broke its back.

All told, he'd sunk five small ships adding up to 1,500 tons. Not a big haul but not bad for a night's work. The men had earned their beer.

"That was … savage," Hooker said.

Charlie acknowledged this comment with a grim nod. *Savage*, yes. The perfect word for it. He leaned against the coaming, venting the stress of battle and three weeks of frustration with a ragged sigh.

"Conn, Bridge," he said. "Set a course for Borongan."

At Borongan in the north, they'd try their luck again. Charlie hoped to catch more Japanese merchants as they fled Third Fleet.

"Captain, we can't go there," Rusty replied.

"Explain."

"We received a flash message from Pearl. We have new orders."

CHAPTER TWENTY-THREE

NEW ORDER

Charlie stepped through the passageway into the chief petty officers' stateroom, where Chief Pharmacist's Mate Henry Pearce operated on the wounded sailor, Signalman Third Class Eddie Kendrick. Still wearing his flak jacket, Morrison's face was anxious and blackened with gunpowder.

"How is he, Doc?" Charlie said.

Concentrating on his stitching, Pearce grunted but otherwise didn't answer. Kendrick had taken shrapnel in his right leg. The medic had tied off the bleeders, cleaned the wound with alcohol, and dowsed it with sulfa powder. Kendrick lay clutching a pillow to his chest, in discomfort but feeling little pain thanks to a shot of morphine.

One of the most valuable crewmen, the pharmacist's mate had the same training as a civilian paramedic but served the boat as its doctor, nurse, dentist, and chaplain. Men who smashed their fingers when tossed around the boat in heavy weather, broke a rib clearing the topsides, or caught the clap on shore leave all went to see Doc. When he wasn't treating the crew, he served as a day lookout, the ship's librarian, and part of the cleaning detail for the after battery room. Pearce had kept Charlie alive and nursed him back to health after he'd caught a jungle fever on Saipan.

His stitching done, Pearce cleaned a few of Kendrick's minor wounds with merthiolate, covered them with sterile dressings, and began putting away his instruments. "He'll be all right, but he'll be on the sick list for the duration."

"Thanks, Doc," Charlie said.

"Don't mention it, Captain."

As the pharmacist's mate took his leave, Morrison gazed at Charlie. "It was a shell from the minelayer. Went off right in front of us. A geyser of water shot up. Metal pinged everywhere. I'm amazed only one of us got hit."

"Morrison."

The man's eyes focused. "Captain?"

"You did good. You did right by the *Sandtiger*."

The torpedo officer shivered, no doubt thinking how close he'd come to getting hit, how lucky he was to have avoided it. "Thank you, sir." He let out a bark of laughter. "Careful what you wish for, right?"

Charlie looked down at the wounded sailor, who had fallen asleep due to the morphine. If Kendrick had died, it would have been on him as captain for ordering the attack. Dodging responsibility for a man's death was a different kind of close call. He knew, if one of his men died in combat, it'd chew him up inside. In calling him a navel gazer, Braddock had him pegged, but maybe he was right about another thing, that this made a good commander.

He thought of the Robert E. Lee quote Rusty had told him. How could a good commander order the death of what he loved?

Because he put duty first? Maybe it was because he believed his attack would kill the enemy, not his own men. Maybe because he had no other choice.

Or maybe it was because, if some men died, the rest would live and go home.

Charlie remembered how Rusty had told him on the S-55 that young men had a death wish. Not a real wish to die but a willingness, almost a craving, to face death and survive it. At the time, he'd questioned whether he would be willing to order the death of the thing he loved the most, which was his own life.

To kill the enemy? No.

To make sure his comrades lived? Absolutely. Just as Smokey had.

In any case, he didn't have to think too hard about it right now. The *Sandtiger* had received new orders, and they didn't involve shooting torpedoes.

"We received a new operation order," he told Morrison.

The torpedo officer perked up, which made Charlie smile. He'd had the same reaction when Rusty told him about the new order radioed from Pearl. He'd thought, this was it; there was a big mission related to the invasion, and the *Sandtiger* would play a special role. The boat, like her crew, had her own destiny.

"We're on lifeguard duty," he explained.

"Oh," Morrison said, crestfallen.

No sooner had the submarine officer survived action in which he'd been inches away from being killed or wounded, he wanted to be right back in the thick of it.

Charlie knew exactly how he felt.

Among the submarines, lifeguard duty was important but not particularly desired. It involved a boat being on station during airstrikes and rescuing downed aviators from the sea.

"We're bombing the Philippines then, sir?"

"On the other side of Guiuan Peninsula is Kinkaid's Seventh Fleet," Charlie said. "We aren't just bombing the Philippines. We're invading it."

Morrison perked up again. Though lifeguard

duty wasn't exciting, this particular mission guaranteed a front row seat to a major invasion—and a turning point in the war.

Charlie added, "Third Fleet, meanwhile, is roaming north of us, guarding Seventh's flank and looking for the Japanese."

"I'd rather be with them."

He snorted. "Me too."

At least he'd gotten some action on this patrol, which now threatened to come to a tame finish. Whether pulling lifeguard duty or acting as a picket for a mobile fleet, neither promised much action for a submarine. The boats worked best when they worked alone, in open space, with the element of surprise.

Braddock stomped into the small room. Already cramped, it barely fit the big machinist. "How's he doing?"

"Doc says nothing more than a scar to remember it by," Charlie told him. "Sick list for the rest of the patrol."

"I told Doc to put him in my bunk. I'd like him to stay here until he's good to return to the crew's quarters. I'll hot bunk until then. That all right with you, sir."

That last part a statement, not a question. Braddock was now a mama bear to the enlisted men of the *Sandtiger*, still a misanthrope to everybody else.

"That'll be fine, Chief."

In the crew's mess, the sailors were cheering.

"What's going on?" Morrison said.

Braddock grinned and said, "Beer, sir."

CHAPTER TWENTY-FOUR

LIFEGUARDS

At dawn, the *Sandtiger* cruised in San Pablo Bay, near Tacloban City on the island of Leyte, in a patch of water designated as a ditching station for aviators. Big American flags lay tied to her decks next to the conning tower, clearly designating her as friendly. She was part of Seventh Fleet now, which lay stacked behind her for miles.

Cruisers, dozens of destroyers, both American and Australian, an incredible display of military might. The battleships *Maryland*, *West Virginia*, *Tennessee*, *California*, and *Pennsylvania*, salvaged after the brutal assault on Pearl Harbor three years ago. Light carriers launching planes. And behind them, more than 400 amphibious craft carrying four divisions of the U.S. Sixth Army.

General Douglas MacArthur had promised the people of the Philippines he'd return, and he seemed intent on keeping his word.

From the *Sandtiger*'s bridge, Charlie and Rusty

scanned the shoreline with binoculars. Rollers broke against yellow beaches backed by green jungle. A strange thing, cruising on the surface during the day in sight of a Japanese stronghold.

A wave of fifty American planes roared overhead. P-51 Mustangs, F6F Hellcats, and other fighters and dive bombers. They swept over the gulf's pale blue waters, following the rollers.

"It's begun," Charlie said.

Within hours, thousands of GIs would storm the beaches.

"Ironic, isn't it, Skipper," Rusty said.

"What's that?"

"Playing lifeguard for the guys who bombed our boat and tried to kill us."

Charlie was still chafing at the new order attaching him to Admiral Kincaid. "Don't forget they strafed us in the Battle of the Philippine Sea too."

"War may be hell, but sometimes it's funny," Rusty said. "Funny in a 'haha, you dodged a bullet right onto a landmine' kind of way."

Charlie smiled, drinking in the briny scent of the bay, the engines pulsing, the palm trees crowding the shoreline. "Remember this. Just take a moment to let it all sink in."

"Skipper?"

"This is a big moment. This operation might end the war." And was far bigger than his ambition to sink another ship or two before his patrol ended. "When we take the Philippines back, we'll cut off the Japs from the rest of their empire. They'll surrender, if they know what's good for them."

Rusty snorted. "They don't."

The planes reached for land. The coastal treeline stood still in dawn's pale light. If the Japanese were there, they were hiding. The heaviest formation raced toward Tacloban airfield, which lay along the Cataisan Peninsula.

Then sparks erupted from the earth, tracer rounds from AA guns streaking toward the American planes. Charlie raised his binoculars again for a better look. Puffs of black smoke erupted in the sky. The formation dissolved as individual planes broke off to dive toward ground targets.

A cluster of Japanese Zeros rose from the airfield to challenge the invaders. Charlie watched them dance with his heart in his throat, wincing as planes flamed out of the blue. From here, he couldn't tell which planes were American.

"We're in it now," Rusty told the lookouts. "Keep a sharp eye."

Charlie's AA gun crews aimed the big guns

at the sky. While the carrier planes were sup-posed to protect the *Sandtiger*, he wasn't taking any chances with a Zero breaking through and making a run at him.

Their ordnance spent, the American planes streamed back to their carriers as a fresh wave howled over the island.

Then the battleships opened fire with their fourteen-inch guns.

"Yeah," Rusty grinned. "This is it."

The force of the great thudding blasts echoed through the *Sandtiger*'s hull. The massive shells sounded like freight trains pounding overhead, which Charlie remembered all too well from his adventures on Saipan.

This time, the awesome firepower was going the other way, and he couldn't help but smile too. "I asked Morrison what he thought of his first war patrol."

"What did he say?" Rusty said.

"He said it was like a movie, but he was in it."

The exec laughed. "You want to know what it feels like to me?"

"What?"

"Winning."

The shells struck the island, one earthshaking rumble after another that hurled vast hills of dirt and splintered trees high into the air. Columns of smoke poured into the sky from the airfield and other points across the island.

Charlie leaned on the coaming. "Did you ever think we'd end up here?"

"After Cavite, I can't believe I'm here at all. I honestly didn't think we'd survive that first year, much less end up giving the Japs hell."

When the war started, Rusty had been serving on the S-55, stationed as part of the Asiatic Fleet at Cavite Navy Yard, the Philippines. Three days after the Pearl Harbor attack, the Japanese bombed the base and flattened it. In the war's first year, America barely held on in the Pacific, and the submarines had been largely ineffective at stopping the Japanese juggernaut.

"We've had a hell of a ride," Charlie said.

"We're winning, but it isn't over yet. It's bad luck to talk like we're all going home. It isn't over by a long shot. The Japs just won't quit."

Maybe he was right. The United States wouldn't quit until they'd gained Japan's unconditional surrender. The Japanese leadership would never agree to that unless they felt they had no choice. Until then, many more sailors and soldiers on both sides would lose life and limb because the Japanese would fight to impose a high enough cost that the Americans would negotiate for peace.

Rusty added, "I have a bad feeling we'll be fighting them on their home islands soon enough. And I'll be glad I'm not a GI."

During Charlie's patrol in the Sea of Japan, Lt. Tanaka had told him the Japanese would never surrender, that they'd fight to the last man for their emperor. If that were true, the bloodbath was still only getting started, a depressing thought. He hated the idea this might go on for another three years.

"Plane, near, approaching!" one of the lookouts said.

Charlie focused on a plane that was trailing smoke. "Ours or theirs?"

"Ours, I think," Rusty answered. "He shoots at us, so help me, I'll yank him out of the water myself and knock him flat on his can."

The plane was a Wildcat, flying half blind because of the black smoke pouring from its engine, its wings riddled with holes from a flak burst. The engine coughed. Without power, the propeller windmilled.

The plane glided into the bay and slammed into the water. The pilot struggled to exit the shattered canopy. The hot engine sizzled in a cloud of steam.

"All ahead emergency!" Charlie ordered.

The helmsman rang up flank speed on both annunciators. The overloaded engines howled and spewed black smoke from the vents. The submarine gained speed, closing on the wreck. The pilot stood on the plane, pulled the toggles to inflate his Mae West with carbon dioxide, and waved.

The Wildcat pitched forward and started to go under nose first, tail hook in the air. It sank like a rock, leaving the pilot floundering in the water.

Charlie conned the boat near the fighter pilot and ordered all stop on the engines. The *Sandtiger* coasted alongside him. The man was too waterlogged and exhausted to climb the steps on the side of the boat. Two sailors dropped into the water to help him onto the boat and up to the bridge.

The pilot sketched a salute and said, "Second Lieutenant George Jackson, Air Squadron VC-4 assigned to CVE-66, the *White Plains*. Am I glad to see you!"

"Welcome aboard the *Sandtiger*," Charlie said. "I'm Lt. Commander Charlie Harrison, and this is Rusty, our exec. He'll take you below and get you set up with some brandy and hot coffee."

"I was flying at 20,000 feet and ran into a wall of flak," the pilot went on in a daze. "Dove on a target to attack before climbing again. That's when I found out I'd been hit. I lost power but kept climbing on momentum. After that, I just couldn't keep altitude." His eyes flickered and focused on Charlie's face. "Did you say you got liquor on this ship?"

"Waiting for you below." Rusty held out his hand. "First, I'll need to take your sidearm and any ammunition you have on you."

The pilot handed over his .38. "What happens after that?"

Charlie said, "We'll get you back to your ship soon enough. Until then, go dry off, grab a drink, learn how to use the head, and then get back here."

"You want me back? For what?"

"You're going to help keep us alive, Lieutenant."

CHAPTER TWENTY-FIVE

THE RESCUE

The battleships pounded Leyte while American planes dominated the skies. A handful of Japanese planes broke through and managed to damage a few ships. One of the attacks was a suicide. Otherwise, the contest remained one-sided. The lookouts called out every contact. Charlie grew increasingly tense as the battle raged.

Dressed in blue shirt and dungarees, Lt. Jackson returned with Rusty. The pilot's rapid exit and sour expression suggested he was grateful to escape the submarine's heat, stink, and cramped spaces where he was in everybody's way.

"What am I supposed to call you?" he asked.

"On this ship, I'm addressed as 'Captain.'"

"Well, Captain, what do you want me to do?"

"Can you tell the enemy's planes from ours at a distance?"

"My life depends on me doing just that."

Charlie handed him a pair of binoculars. "You're hired."

There wasn't much to see now. American planes were swarming back to their carriers, and the next wave was still far off. The lull in air cover made him nervous. Then the planes reached the island, and he breathed easier.

"Captain," a lookout said. "Multiple landing craft, bearing two-eight-oh, range 5,000 yards, approaching!"

Charlie checked his watch: 1000. The battleships and carrier planes had been at it for four hours. Now Seventh Fleet was ready to land the grunts.

Over three hundred feet long and weighing 1,800 tons, more than 150 "landing ship, tank" type craft growled toward shore at twelve knots, each loaded with 150 soldiers. Though slow and clumsy, the LSTs could take a lot of damage and remain afloat. Their large ballast systems could be flooded for a deep draft or blown to allow them to sail very close to beaches.

With large bow waves, the LSTs plodded toward the shoreline, while the battleships' great guns silenced. Small splashes geysered from the bay as enemy mortars opened up. Charlie winced as a shell struck a crowded LST with a burst of debris and bodies. Then the landing craft reached the beach and yawned open.

Columns of soldiers poured forward rifles first and pounded sand.

He gripped the coaming, expecting a slaughter-house.

In this first wave, more than 20,000 men raced across the beaches and into the jungle, concentrated along a four-mile stretch of beach between Tacloban airfield and the Palo River, and a three-mile stretch to the south between San José and the Daguitan River. Despite sporadic gunfire, resistance seemed to be far lighter than what the Marines encountered on Saipan. Charlie was relieved.

The Navy and the carrier planes' bombardment had effectively softened up the enemy. The pillboxes within view stood empty. The Japanese had withdrawn.

The LSTs backed from the beach, one of them still smoking from a mortar hit, and lurched to return for more troops. As the GIs pressed inland and established a beachhead, the first vehicles would be offloaded.

And hospital units and equipment.

Charlie wondered if Jane would end up here sewing up GIs. Knowing her, she probably was aboard one of those ships. Like him, Jane always wanted to go where the action was.

"One of our planes is having trouble," Jackson said.

Charlie grimaced. The fighter pilot was a better lookout than he was, staying focused on observing rather than thinking about a particular tantalizing Army nurse.

The man pointed to a distant speck in the sky, which appeared to be losing altitude to the northwest. "There, see? It's a turkey."

Charlie raised his binoculars. "A what?"

"An Avenger. They're turkeys compared to the Wildcats."

"Uh-huh. He's falling fast. Is he going to make it into the bay?"

"He'll make it, but it's going to be close."

"Helm, come right twenty-five degrees," Charlie ordered. "All ahead emergency."

Again, the maneuvering and engine rooms responded with quick efficiency, propelling the *Sandtiger* forward on all four mains.

"He's going to land in the harbor," the pilot said.

Charlie didn't like the looks of it. Bad odds out there. "If he does, we'll be exposed to shore batteries. One good hit, and we're done."

"We still have to try."

"He's down," Rusty said. "In the harbor, just like Jackson said. Three crew are getting out and inflating a raft."

Tacloban Harbor was surrounded by Tacloban City to the west, Burayan to the south, and

Cataisan Peninsula and its airfield to the east. Entering it, the *Sandtiger* would be exposed to guns shooting at her from three sides.

"Please, Captain," Jackson pleaded.

Charlie knew he had to try. He thought through his options and came to a decision. "We've got a powerful radio setup on this boat. Talk to your people and arrange for some air cover, and we'll go in and get your guys."

Jackson grinned. "Wilco! Thank you."

Hooker took the man below. Charlie turned to Rusty, who was staring at him. "I know, I know, I'm a damned fool."

"Actually, I'm glad we're doing it," his friend said. "It's worth the risk."

"I'm glad you think so."

"It can't always be about killing Japs. Sometimes, we have to put ourselves on the line to save Americans."

"It's the same thing to me," Charlie said.

"Then we should do it. This particular job is risk, reward, and responsibility all rolled into one."

"Yeah," he agreed, though he still didn't like it. It was one thing to approach an enemy harbor submerged or while surfaced at night. In broad daylight, with the enemy alert and out for blood, was pure craziness. "Conn, Bridge."

"Go ahead, Bridge."

"Battle stations, gun action. Stand by to rig for collision."

"Aye, Captain."

Morrison and his gun crew piled from the gun hatch and set up the deck gun. "Ready to fire, Captain!"

"Very well. Stand by."

The *Sandtiger* rounded Cataisan Point. The Japanese troops at the airfield had their hands full fighting X Corps, too busy to even notice the submarine cruising past. They didn't fire a single shot at the boat.

The air hummed.

Jackson emerged from the hatch and grinned at the sound. "That's our escort."

The planes zoomed overhead, rocking their wings in greeting.

"Good thinking, getting them in the game," Rusty said. "We've got our own air force now."

"Better than them trying to sink us again," Charlie said.

"What do you mean?" the pilot said.

Charlie and Rusty exchanged a smile. "Never mind. Long story."

The pilots were paddling their raft hard toward the bay. Mortar shells splashed around them. The planes dove toward the flashes, dropping ordnance. AA fire arced into the sky.

Charlie watched it all with mounting anxiety. "I hope we don't have to rescue anybody else." Mostly, he was hoping his decision to get the carrier planes involved didn't result in any of them getting killed.

"Don't worry about them," Jackson said. "They know what they're doing, and why they're doing it. They won't leave a man behind."

"All compartments, rig for collision," Charlie ordered.

The *Sandtiger* knifed across the harbor, racing for the airmen. The sea erupted around them as the enemy gunners switched targets. The deck gun banged at a distant shore battery.

"Helm, swing us around so we're downwind of the raft," Charlie said. The same maneuver used when a sailor fell overboard.

The Avenger had a crew of three, the pilot, turret gunner, and a radioman/bombardier. The raft bobbed in waters churned up by the shelling. The *Sandtiger*'s deck rose and fell on the swells.

As submarine and raft began to converge, he yelled, "All stop!"

A shell struck close aboard, rocking the submarine. Lacking the submariners' sea legs, Jackson tumbled to the deck with a cry.

"Throw them a line!" Charlie said.

The sailors hurled a line at the raft and pulled the airmen aboard.

"They're aboard! Helm, left full rudder! All ahead emergency! Go, go, go!"

Another shell hurled a wave of water across the deck as the *Sandtiger* made for the relative safety of the bay. One by one, the planes broke contact and returned to their carriers, rocking their wings in farewell. Morrison fired one last round before securing the gun.

Then the rapid operation was over. The airmen rescued, no casualties. A small success but an important one.

"Thank you, Captain," Jackson said. "You guys really know your stuff."

Rusty grinned at the dazed airmen who sat gasping on the deck and turned to Charlie. "You know what, Skipper? That was maybe the most personally worthwhile thing I've done in this war."

It was one of the greatest ironies of war that taking life ultimately saved life, but Charlie had to agree. He was tired of the endless killing, and using his boat to save these men from capture or death at the hands of the Japanese gave him far more satisfaction than he thought it would.

Still, as he leaned against the bridge coaming, his legs trembled with spent adrenaline. Rusty was right, it was unlucky to think about the war being over and going home. Not because he believed in superstitions, but because he'd allowed something he'd forbade himself for three years.

Hope.

CHAPTER TWENTY-SIX

HEY, TARGETS

The *Sandtiger* patrolled throughout the day until her crew was ordered to stand down and return to station off Samar's coast. She cruised between hundreds of American ships of all shapes and sizes, finally stopping near a destroyer, the *McNair*. In so doing, she missed witnessing General MacArthur make his dramatic return through Leyte's surf to again stand on Philippine soil.

Charlie and Rusty shook hands with the airmen, a happy bunch who would receive a hero's welcome when they returned to their carriers.

"Thanks again, guys," Jackson said. "In the future, I'll be looking twice before I open up on any submarines."

"You do that," Rusty said. "We got enough problems."

"Tell me about it. Based on the stink down there, I might be doing you favor if I did shoot."

Charlie chuckled. "Good luck, Lieutenant. We still have a ways to go before we can go home."

The men clambered into a raft. Hooker and another sailor wielded the oars.

"Hey, bubbleheads!" a man called from the *McNair*. "Thanks for showing up!"

"Hey yourselves, targets!" Rusty called back. "Thanks for taking our riders!"

The sailors on both ships laughed at the good-natured exchange. Even the *McNair*'s stern patrician captain, standing on his bridge, cracked a smile.

Rusty turned to Charlie. "So what's next, Skipper?"

"Seven days, and we're going home. I figured we'd try our luck at Borongan, then head north and see what we see."

"My bet is the Japs hightailed it."

A safe bet. In fact, no Japanese skipper in his right mind would bring a merchantman anywhere near Area Twenty now. The *Sandtiger* carried enough fuel to extend the patrol a few days beyond that, but there likely wouldn't be any point.

"We're probably in for a quiet week," Charlie admitted.

"We earned it."

"How are we set for beer? I'm wondering if we serve the rest out tonight, whether I'll finally be able to take a shower."

"It might be worth a shot," Rusty said. "Me, I'll be busy reviewing department reports. Always paperwork to be done for the CO."

Charlie chuckled. "He's a real bastard, from what I hear."

"'*Hara-kiri*,' they call him."

"The scourge of the seven seas. Sank a coaster."

Rusty smiled into the wind. "You did just fine, brother."

"I hope ComSubPac thinks so."

"It doesn't matter. I'm telling you that you did just fine."

Charlie wasn't the type of man to ever believe he did just fine, but he appreciated hearing it from Rusty.

"We did all right this patrol, I guess."

The *Sandtiger* had missed the *Mamiya*, braved a typhoon, and nearly sank after being bombed by her own country's carrier planes. But she'd sunk several enemy ships and rescued four airmen under fire.

And most important, she and her crew had survived to fight another day.

"Let's get a cup of coffee," Rusty said. "I'm buying."

With a final wave to the departing airmen, they went below. Charlie gave the conn to Nixon and passed through the control room, where Spike informed him the boat and her crew were running tip top. Despite her age and scars, the *Sandtiger* had pulled through time and again on the patrol, as had her able crew. Morale was up. Maybe Rusty was right, and he'd done all right by them.

He led Rusty into the wardroom, where Percy sat on the bench behind the table, tuning his five-string banjo in open G.

"Just the man I wanted to see," Charlie said.

The communications officer stopped. "What did I do now?"

Charlie removed his harmonica from his breast pocket. "Start us off."

Percy grinned and did a forward roll to test his instrument's sound. "Jimmie Davis, 'You Are My Sunshine.' One, two, three..."

He dove right into the song. Charlie puckered up and joined in with his harmonica while Rusty took out his fiddle from where he'd stowed it.

Then Percy began to sing in his lonesome voice. Halfway through, Charlie heard the off-duty chiefs sing along in their stateroom aft of the wardroom, and then the forward torpedomen. Waldron brought more coffee and joined in.

Each of Charlie's former captains had used an activity to pass the time and build camaraderie among his officers. For Kane, it was chess. Hunter, hearts. Moreau, poker. Whether focused more on skill or chance, these games sharpened instincts through competition.

For Charlie, it was music. He bonded with his officers through melodic collaboration. As with a good piece of music, a submarine's crew had to come together to produce perfect harmony.

This time, however, the song made him feel lonely, a strange thing on a crowded boat. It wasn't just the loneliness of command. He missed Evie and Jane, wondered when he'd see them again. The ties to home he'd severed when he'd joined the Submarine Force had begun to reassert themselves.

The tune came to a close.

"Goddamn, that song makes me homesick," Percy said.

"I know what you mean," Rusty said.

"That's a good thing for me, Exec."

"How so?"

The communications officer said, "I'm starting to think I might actually get there." He glanced down at his ridiculous Aloha shirt. "Moreau…"

Percy didn't have to voice his deep fears. His lucky shirts, his hard drinking, his nightmares were all born while serving under the highly aggressive Captain Moreau. He'd feared *Hara-kiri* might be cut in the same bloodthirsty, risk-taking image.

Right now, he was saying he trusted Charlie to balance aggression with the crew's safety. That he trusted Charlie to get him home.

Sitting in awkward silence, Charlie didn't know what to say to that. Rusty saved the day by launching into Nat King Cole's "D-Day," a song about the Allied invasion of Hitler's Europe back in June, which had occurred while Charlie had been fighting on Saipan. Before he'd returned to sea for his current patrol, the Allies were steadily advancing toward Germany's Siegfried Line, and the Soviets had captured Bucharest.

The *Sandtiger's* hum changed in pitch, as if she too wished to have a part in playing the patriotic song. Charlie felt her moving. The airmen had been safely delivered to the *McNair*, and she was heading north back into Area Twenty. She was through with being a lifeguard. Soon, she'd return to the hunt.

Whatever the respite and no matter how long, the war always waited.

CHAPTER TWENTY-SEVEN

A GOOD PATROL

Five days later, on October 24, the weather-beaten *Sandtiger* cruised on two mains east of the Samar port town of Gamay. Her crew followed their routines and thought about their upcoming liberty in Honolulu. They greased the torpedo tubes, checked gravity in the battery cells, tested for grounds in the electrical circuits, and all the other important but typical activities needed to keep the iron lady on patrol.

Feeling clean for the first time in over a month, Charlie entered the crew's mess. He'd finally found time to take a shower, if one could call those seconds of frantic soaping and rinsing a real shower, and he'd shaved his beard. He'd put on a fresh khaki uniform for the occasion, which was to mark the end of the patrol. In just two days, the *Sandtiger* would return to port.

Officers and crew cheered his arrival while Harry James's "I've Heard That Song Before" played over the 1MC. In their view, he'd done all right. He'd found enemy ships, steered them out of trouble, and led them in a surprise surface attack that resulted in sinkings. And he would get them back to base alive.

None of it compared to the remarkable deeds Charlie had accomplished before. He'd once sunk an aircraft carrier, the kind of achievement that made more than one skipper's career. But that was the past. Now he was captain, and he didn't have to be Superman to be a good one. He just had to be good at his job, deal as much damage as he could when he found the Japanese, and get his men back safely.

He raised his hands for quiet. "We'll be heading back to base soon, and I just wanted to say it was an honor leading you men on this patrol. They say submarining is a team sport, and you proved it. Things were quieter than I'd like this time out, but we did all right by the Navy and our families back home. If they were here tonight in the flesh, as they are in spirit, I know they'd be plenty proud of all of us. The invasion of the Philippines is the beginning of the end for the Japs. Soon, we'll all be back with our families again."

The crew cheered again. Even John Braddock, sitting at one of the tables, cracked a smile.

Charlie added, "To say thanks for doing your duty to the utmost, Mr. Nixon worked up a special treat for tonight's meal. Mr. Nixon?"

"Thank you, Captain." The engineering officer's cheeks flushed as all eyes switched to him. "I, uh, rebuilt the ice cream freezer in the control room. It's been—"

The sailors cut him off with a roar, pounding the tables. Ice cream makers were the kind of luxury limited to battleship wardrooms. Saunders's order to dismantle the last one Nixon had built had been distinctly unpopular.

Nixon blinked at them, reddening further. "I installed it in the control room and hooked it up to the main refrigeration system. A motor automatically cranks it—"

Charlie put a hand on the man's shoulder, urging him to speed it along. The crew was practically drooling.

"It's peach melba," Nixon finished. "Chief Sullivan was a big help—"

The men roared again as the cooks served up gobs of melting ice cream in soup bowls. They devoured it in seconds and asked for more, though the cooks were saving the rest for the next rotation coming in for their dinner.

"Yum," Rusty said. "Peach with a diesel oil aftertaste."

Charlie laughed, eyeing the crew. "They don't seem to mind."

Nixon smiled as well. "I'm going to miss this, Captain."

"You will?"

The engineering officer could handle bureaucracy and machinery. The company of other men, not so much. Charlie had never gotten the sense Nixon cared for any of it. He and the Navy didn't seem particularly cut out for each other.

"I know I'm not a typical guy," Nixon said. "I have a hard time with people. When I get home, I'll never have friends like this again. This boat is like a family to me. I'll miss it."

"You know," Charlie said. "I think I know exactly what you mean."

"I'm ready to go home," Rusty said.

"I know exactly what you mean too. I hope this war ends soon. Still, all this is going to be hard to leave behind. For me, it isn't just the crew. It's everything about command. Nothing back in the real world is ever going to compare."

"Told you you'd grow into the job," Rusty said.

Nixon talked to the chief cook, who handed him another bowl of ice cream. "For Kendrick," he told Charlie. "I figured he could use a boost."

"Good thinking," Charlie said. "You're a good man, Nix."

The engineering officer narrowed his eyes at Braddock, who caught him looking and returned a grudging nod of respect. "I'm the best."

Nixon carried the ice cream off to Kendrick. Charlie left as well, heading aft to take the *Sandtiger's* pulse. He passed through the cluttered crew's quarters, the bunks and lockers bolted into the bulkhead among piping and hanging baggage. Then into the hot and loud engine compartments, navigating the narrow path between the massive, pulsing Fairbanks Morse engines. Then through Maneuvering to Aft Torpedo and back forward, all the way to the control room, which was crammed with pipes, valves, and gauges. Everywhere he went was filled with sweating men and noise and the diesel stench.

In the wardroom, he passed the time with his harmonica before deciding to turn in. Lying in his bunk, he replayed the patrol in his mind, already framing the report for Cooper, and surprised himself by agreeing with every decision he'd made and the assessment he'd given the crew. Quieter than he'd wanted, yes, but they'd done their duty and achieved some good.

For the first time in weeks, he didn't fret over outcomes he couldn't control and fell asleep quickly.

He was treading water in the middle of the vast blue Pacific while Evie paddled toward him in a raft. He wondered how long he could hold on. As the raft approached, he raised his hand.

She reached to pull him from the water—

A hand shook him awake. "Sorry to wake you, Captain."

The voice belonged to Yeoman Lucas.

Charlie sat up and rubbed his eyes. The dream came back to him, and he shuddered. "You did me a favor. What's up, Yeo?"

The time was 0356. He'd slept for a solid seven hours.

Lucas offered him a mug of coffee. "Mr. Percy wanted me to tell you there's a battle going on down by Leyte."

He took the mug, slurped it, and handed it back. "Thanks, Yeo."

Fighting to the south meant the Japanese were launching a night attack on the island, or it might mean something else.

It might mean the Imperial Japanese Navy's Combined Fleet was attacking.

CHAPTER TWENTY-EIGHT

ARMADA

Charlie mounted to the bridge. Under the cover of darkness, the *Sandtiger* knifed due east on a glassy sea. The night was a hot eighty degrees and humid. Thick patches of cloud cover blacked out parts of the starry sky.

He said to Rusty, "Couldn't sleep again?"

"Bad dream," Rusty said. "I came up here for the air, and all of a sudden, there's a battle going on." Rusty pointed. "There."

Flashes popped along the southern horizon, bringing Samar's hilly outline into stark silhouette. Booms thudded in the distance.

The flashes died out.

"I can't tell if that's Sixth Army's artillery or Seventh Fleet," Charlie said.

"Or bomber planes," Rusty noted.

"No hum." If it were bombers, they'd have heard the propellers.

New arcs of yellow light flared and faded

except for a glowing smear where ships had fired starshells to light up the night.

The thunder rolled over them moments later.

"Christ, that's battleships," Rusty said. "Can you hear it?"

The Imperial Japanese Navy had finally made its move to counter the invasion of Leyte. Skilled at night fighting, the Japanese ships were trying to get at the American invasion shipping and isolate Sixth Army on the island.

"I hope Seventh Fleet is giving more than it's getting."

"They're getting revenge, brother."

Seventh Fleet included battleships raised from the harbor at Pearl. Repaired, refurbished, and put back in action after the attack that started the war.

Charlie chafed at the distance. With no real idea what was happening, he considered his options for bringing the *Sandtiger* into the fight, all of which involved getting the submarine around the third largest island in the Philippines before dawn.

He wanted to swing around Samar, cross the Visayan Sea, and get behind the Japanese to pick off damaged ships limping from the fight. He checked the time. After 0400. The trek would take around seven hours running on the surface, which he didn't dare to do in these waters during the day.

In any case, the battle would likely be long over by the time he got there.

He was right there less than a week ago. He had no luck!

The only viable path forward was to maintain course, steam down the coast, and come in behind Seventh Fleet. They could reach Leyte Gulf in three hours. There, he could re-examine his options.

"What do you want to do?" Rusty said.

"We'll maintain our present—"

"Contact!" one of the lookouts cried. "Ships, approaching, far, bearing three-double-oh."

Charlie wheeled. "That must be Third Fleet. Some of their ships should be guarding the San Bernardino Strait."

Kinkaid's Seventh Fleet was the invasion fleet, and Admiral Bull Halsey's Third Fleet was the operation's roaming offensive arm.

Eyes glued to his binoculars, Rusty shrugged. He knew as much as Charlie did.

Charlie searched but couldn't find them. Perched on the shears, the lookouts were at a greater height than him, able to see a little farther.

"Conn, Bridge," he said. "Helm, reduce speed to one-third. All stop."

The *Sandtiger* coasted until her forward momentum bled out.

"All back, full," Charlie ordered.

The submarine's engines rumbled as she overcame inertia and began to reverse. Soon, he was able to discern a series of black smudges from the surrounding darkness.

Warships, hull-down on the horizon.

All the while on the other side of Samar, guns boomed as battleships pounded each other in the night. Charlie felt like a mouse scurrying between massive elephants searching each other out to grapple in the dark.

Just enough star and moonlight for visibility. He identified a fleet of heavy ships on a bearing of one-double-oh. They advanced in three columns at a speed of around ten knots, screened by destroyers and light cruisers.

"They aren't running navigation lights," he said.

Rusty grunted in agreement. "Whatever they're doing, they're trying to do it without anybody knowing they're doing it."

The lookout said, "I don't think they're ours, Captain."

Despite the hot, muggy air, Charlie shivered. He was looking at IJN capital ships on their way to Leyte Gulf.

He said, "Where the hell is Third Fleet?"

"The Japs will be behind Kinkaid in hours," Rusty said.

"Helm, all stop," Charlie ordered.

"Even if Kinkaid beats the Japs in front of him, he'll be strung out and in need of resupply."

"I know."

Rusty waited until he couldn't stand it. "You want to attack, don't you?"

"I was thinking about it."

"Look, if we—"

"But I won't."

"I'm serious—wait. Really? We're not attacking?"

"Attacking won't accomplish anything," he said. "We might sink a ship, maybe two. We'd end up out of action, and it wouldn't stop them or even slow them down much. You have to pick your battles, right?"

"Well," said Rusty. "Okay, then. So how do you want to play it?"

Soon, the enemy ships would pass fairly close. With no bow wake and her low, gray profile against the backdrop of the coast, the *Sandtiger* could observe them while being virtually invisible. The enemy's big surface ships had radar, but the proximity of Samar would scatter the reflections, camouflaging the submarine.

Charlie planned to gather as much information as possible and radio it up the chain of command, per his operation order. Then he'd follow in the enemy's wake and keep sending contact reports until Kinkaid or Halsey reacted.

At which time he'd take his shot.

The *Sandtiger* would be in a perfect position to submerge and send every torpedo she had into damaged ships retreating from the battle.

Submarine skippers would kill to be standing where he was now. He had a well-drilled crew and torpedoes warming up in the tubes, and he was near an IJN task force that didn't know he was there. Few had even been this close.

He remembered Captain Kane, after a string of mishaps led to him sinking multiple convoy targets, saying, *"Sometimes, you get lucky."*

The lesson was you didn't need to be lucky all the time to win. You only needed to get lucky once, when it mattered, and be ready to act on it.

He shared his plan with Rusty before sending him below to radio Pearl and start a tracking party on the enemy fleet. Then he went back to counting ships. The enemy crossed the *Sandtiger*'s beam, filing past thirty miles off Samar's coast. In Charlie's view, just below the horizon.

He estimated the enemy fleet to number at least fifteen ships. Beyond the destroyer screen and two heavy cruisers, he spotted the pagoda masts of four massive battleships cruising in column. The ships plowed across the sea, large bow wakes marking their passage.

Two of them were real monsters, bigger than their fellows.

Rusty returned. "Message received. They're sending it on to Kinkaid."

"I think we just found the *Yamato*."

Navy men across the Pacific often talked about it. They knew it existed. But few had ever seen it, and little was actually known about its capabilities. Built during the war, the *Yamato* remained shrouded in mystery, like some legendary sea monster.

"You're shitting me," the exec said.

"At the rear of the middle column. That has to be the *Yamato*. The one in front of it must be a second ship in the same class."

Rusty clenched his binoculars as he checked them out. "Jesus. That ship's got to be at least 800 feet long."

One thing that was known about the *Yamato* was it carried massive guns with eighteen-inch bores, capable of hurling giant shells over miles. Same as the Meteor, which had wreaked havoc during the Saipan landings.

Kinkaid was in for a pounding. Charlie hoped Third Fleet wasn't too far away. Arcs of light continued to burst and pulse along the southern horizon.

"Conn, Bridge. Helm, all ahead full." Charlie

turned to Rusty. "You'd better get back below and radio an update to Pearl. And Rusty?"

"Captain?"

"Call all key crewmen to relaxed battle stations. I want them ready to jump when we go to general quarters."

Rusty nodded. "Aye, aye, Captain."

Everybody had believed the Battle of the Philippine Sea was to be the *kantai kessen*—the final grand naval battle predicted by Japanese war planners.

They'd been wrong.

Dawn would bring the real thing in all its fury.

CHAPTER TWENTY-NINE

JUGGERNAUT

Trailing behind as close as she dared, the *Sandtiger* paced the enemy fleet on a southeasterly course along Samar's coast.

Charlie decided not to risk using the radar, which might signal their presence to the Japanese. He and Rusty counted twenty-two warships. Four battleships in the middle column, with four heavy cruisers a couple miles away to port and two to starboard. Destroyers and light cruisers screened the flanks.

Below deck, the crewmembers on duty buzzed with the news they were tracking a Japanese battle fleet.

Rusty rubbed his tired eyes. "Daylight soon."

The battle in the south had lasted only eighteen minutes, and Charlie still had no idea what was happening.

"Where's our fleet?" he growled.

"Maybe the message isn't getting through."

The plan was to submerge in the enemy's track when the American fleet started shooting. So far, however, nobody had shown up.

When dawn arrived, he'd either have to dive or go over the hill, beyond the enemy's horizon.

"Conn, Bridge," he said. "Helm, come left to one-double-oh."

The *Sandtiger* veered to port while edging over twenty knots, squeezing extra speed by keeping the blowers going even though the ballast tanks were dry. She passed north of the slower Japanese formation and dropped over the hill.

"I'm going below to see what I can find out on the scope," Charlie said.

They slid down the hatch into the conning tower. With the crew expecting action, the atmosphere was electric. He shook his head at Percy, hoping he'd pass the word they were still observers in this battle. Then he conned the boat until she was far ahead of the Japanese position.

He said, "Range to the enemy track?"

The answer told him he was now fourteen miles ahead of the IJN fleet.

"Very well," he said. "Have the lookouts clear the shears." This done, he said, "Up scope."

A trick he'd learned from another skipper at the O-Club. Raising the periscope while surfaced enabled the skipper to see farther, so the submarine could keep the enemy in contact while doing an end-around.

Tonight, it would help him find his own fleet.

He crouched and followed the observation scope as it slid from its well, extending the range of his vision from 15,000 to 21,000 yards.

Blackness at first, turning gray. Like the Japanese, the sun was over the hill but coming fast. With the horizon fuzzy in the first light, dawn was a difficult time for observation. He finally discerned a shape, a boxy American ship called a jeep carrier. Basically, a merchantman with a flight deck. Part of Seventh Fleet, these compact flattops launched planes to support the ground troops fighting on Leyte.

He found a second ship and magnified the view. A destroyer escort screening this light carrier task force. Then he spotted two more baby flattops, steaming slowly westward toward Leyte Gulf from their seaward night stations.

Right into the IJN armada.

They had no idea they were sailing to their own annihilation.

Thinly armored, slow, weakly gunned, and carrying a small number of planes equipped with munitions ideal for attacks on ground targets, not surface ships. With typical Navy gallows humor, their sailors claimed the ship's prefix, CVE, stood for combustible, vulnerable, and expendable.

"What's going on?" Rusty said. "You look like you saw Davy Jones."

"They don't know," Charlie muttered.

"What?"

He turned from the scope to glare at his friend. "I'm looking at a task force of escort carriers. They have no idea the IJN is coming."

Rusty shook his head. "Trust me, Skipper. Keep looking."

Charlie returned his attention to the scope.

The rising sun pierced the Philippine Sea like a blinding spear.

He saw everything.

Thick cumulus clouds partially covered the sky. The sea was calm. Scattered rainsqualls grayed out part of his view.

Otherwise, he spotted only CVEs, a few destroyers and destroyer escorts.

Maybe Kinkaid was still bringing his ships up from the south after the short, furious night battle in the gulf.

But if the admiral knew what was going on, why would he allow his light carriers to steam right into the IJN's path?

None of it made sense, unless you assumed the worst.

"I don't see any other ships," Charlie said. "There's nothing to stop the Japanese. I'm telling you, they didn't get our message."

Around him, the crew hunched at their stations, the atmosphere now thick with mounting tension and horror as what was happening out there sank in.

Everything was at risk. The transports, the beachhead on Leyte. The Japanese would easily eliminate the slower jeep carriers. In three hours, they'd smash their way into the gulf and blow the American invasion shipping out of the water.

Wait—the carriers were turning. He zeroed in on one that was launching planes into the wind, an act of necessity. Caught by utter surprise, the task force's commander knew he was in trouble. East was his only escape route.

The sea around the carrier erupted in bright colors.

Dye-colored shells. One of the Japanese battleships had fired a spotting salvo upon which the enemy squadrons could determine the range.

Charlie swung the periscope, and there the Japanese ships were, just coming over the horizon. They'd fired with precision from a range of over ten miles. The heavy ships steamed in column, smoke billowing from their large stacks.

The destroyers and light cruisers raced from the flanks like the horns of a bull, already reaching out to gore the surprised Americans.

CHAPTER THIRTY

COMMAND DECISION

Charlie watched in horror as the Japanese juggernaut closed on the American ships. The sailors around him flinched at the boom of the guns, which reverberated through the *Sandtiger*'s hull.

"Tell us what's happening," Rusty begged.

"The Japanese just delivered a spotting salvo like a textbook example of good gunnery. The carriers are making a run for it."

Another salvo straddled the carrier, which lurched, damaged by the blasts. Its planes continued to take off in frantic lunges. As the tropical sun spilled across the open sea, more carriers came into view. At least a dozen, all lumbering east and billowing heavy smoke from their stacks to camouflage themselves.

The Japanese were firing regularly now, rumbling like thunder.

"The tin cans are laying smoke," he said. "I count only seven in the screen. The carriers are getting every plane they have off their backs. The northernmost are moving into a rainsquall to hide. I still don't see any help coming."

Percy was sending a desperate report to Pearl.

The Japanese fire tapered as they lost visibility of their prey. They continued to advance, their foe's destruction temporarily delayed. The Japanese fleet was faster than the American carriers. It was only a matter of time.

With each passing minute, they closed the distance. With each salvo, improved their accuracy.

Charlie swung the periscope toward the IJN ships. The two giants, the biggest battleships in the world, cruised in his view. One flew the admiral's flag. The armada's flagship.

That ship could only be the *Yamato*.

He turned from the scope. "Helm, come right to one-eight-oh."

The helmsman: "Come right to one-eight-oh, aye, Captain."

The men stared at him, their faces pale in the conning tower's electric lighting.

Rusty said, "What are you thinking, Skipper?"

He wiped the sheen of sweat from his forehead. "I don't know. I don't know what we can do. But I know we can't do a damned thing sitting here. We're going to get a little closer and see if any options present themselves."

He returned to the scope. The American DDs were still firing smoke shells. The smokescreen thickened on the water, covering the carriers that continued to crawl east toward safety.

But not fast enough. The horns of the Japanese bull were already corralling the carriers, pushing them south toward Leyte Gulf where they'd be destroyed.

Or, just as bad, caught in the pincer and swept into the path of the oncoming battleships.

Charlie would have a front row seat to a massacre, and there wasn't anything he could do about it.

He started in surprise. "One of our DDs is attacking. He's charging the Japanese battle line by himself."

The men didn't cheer. They kept working in silence, hanging on Charlie's every word. A single destroyer going up against an IJN fleet, against the likes of the *Yamato*, was suicidal. He doubted it would buy much time for the carriers to escape.

"The DD's firing with his five-inch guns. He hit a heavy cruiser!"

This time, the crew let out a brief cheer.

"Now he's wheeling. He's heading back into the smoke. Wait. The cruiser's on fire. The DD hit him with torpedoes!"

Another cheer, this one louder, more confident. Charlie had served on a destroyer and knew what they could do. While the smallest of the major surface vessels, they could deliver more punch per ton than any other ship type.

The heroic destroyer came out of the smoke again and immediately took a terrible pounding. Debris flew off the superstructure as the ship suffered multiple hits. But it stayed afloat, defiant, guns blazing.

The IJN had made a mistake. Expecting to fight battleships and big aircraft carriers, they were firing armor-piercing rounds, which passed straight through the destroyer's thin armor without exploding.

Having sustained significant damage, the destroyer limped into a rainsquall. Guns flashed in the murk as it continued to engage multiple targets.

And that was that. So much for resistance.

Then the other two destroyers and four destroyer escorts barreled from the smokescreen, launching salvos.

"All the tin cans are in the fight now," Charlie told his excited crew. "They're putting up a hell of a fight."

After several minutes, the first destroyer came out of the squall to attack again. He knew right then what he had to do.

"Down scope."

The crewmen glanced at him in wonder. They didn't want to attack, knowing it would likely end in their sinking. They also couldn't walk away.

He moved to the plotting table, where Percy was tracking the IJN fleet. The other officers gathered around. Whatever action the *Sandtiger* would take, it was his decision alone. Whatever happened, it was his responsibility.

A thin line separated caution and cowardice, heroism and insanity. In Charlie's mind, these lines disappeared. There was only his duty.

He said, "We're going to attack."

If there was any chance of delaying the Japanese long enough for the carriers to escape, for Kinkaid and Halsey to bring up their ships, they had to take it. The prospect terrified him, but he had no choice.

Rusty turned green. This wasn't David versus Goliath. This was more like David fighting Goliath's entire hometown. Charlie expected him to protest, but he didn't.

"Sometimes," the exec said, "you have to pick your battles."

And sometimes, to be a good commander, you had to order the death of that which you loved.

"We have to go in on the surface, but we'll be coming in behind the enemy's DD screen, so we'll still have the element of surprise. There are a lot of planes in the air, so we'll run up our colors and pray those flyboys we rescued don't bomb us again. We're going to go in fast, hit them hard, and dive."

"Great," Percy said with a wince.

"What's the target, Captain?" Morrison said.

"We're going after their flagship. We're going to attack the *Yamato*."

The officers stirred at the idea. If they damaged the enemy's flagship, the attack might stall. It was their best chance to make a difference in the battle's outcome.

The torpedo officer grinned. "Aye, aye."

"Rusty, you'll direct the helm from the topside. Conn us to a ninety-degree track and as close as you can. Morrison, you and your gun crew will have the job of keeping their tin cans away from us. Percy, you'll be diving officer. Nixon, you're going to make sure this old girl does what we ask her to do. Is everybody clear?"

"Aye, aye, Captain," they murmured.

"Then get to your stations." He keyed the 1MC and said, "This is the captain."

His voice blared over speakers throughout the boat.

"By now, you know the Japs are pushing toward Leyte Gulf, and our boys are in big trouble.

The tin cans are putting up one hell of a fight, and now it's our turn. We're going in. We can't walk away from this. Today, we're going to make history. Today, we're going to sink the *Yamato*."

He returned the microphone and said, "Call the men to general quarters. Battle stations, surface attack! Battle stations, gun action!"

CHAPTER THIRTY-ONE

THE HORNET'S NEST

The helmsman gripped the general alarm handle and pulled it out and down. The alarm gonged throughout the boat. All hands rushed to stations.

Charlie mounted to the bridge on trembling legs. He'd always been able to think in a crisis, but right now he was too terrified.

No time for fear. Fear would get him and his crew killed. Half the job of being a good captain was acting the part, even if it meant fooling himself.

Rusty understood as well. He took a deep breath as he joined Charlie on the bridge then set his jaw.

A mild northeasterly wind blew at six knots. Charlie was grateful for the air and space. On the main deck below him, Morrison and his helmeted crew emerged from the gun hatch and unlimbered the five-inch gun, which would be the *Sandtiger*'s only real protection until they got close enough to shoot torpedoes.

"Bridge, Conn," Nixon said over the bridge speaker. "All compartments report battle stations manned. The crew is at general quarters."

On the main deck, Morrison's crew crouched by the five-inch gun. No morale issues there. The torpedo officer had enthusiasm enough for all of them. Additional sailors mounted the 50-caliber and 40-mm Bofors anti-aircraft guns.

"The crew is at general quarters, Captain," Rusty said.

"Very well."

Confident his crew was ready for action, Charlie trained his binoculars ahead. The Japanese ships sprawled on the horizon, steaming south. AA fire filled the sky overhead with tracers and bursts, multicolored like their gun shells to distinguish fire from different ships and help the gunners' accuracy. Hellcats, Helldivers, and Avengers buzzed like hornets, releasing bombs and diving for strafing runs. The bombs they carried were intended to be dropped on ground targets and were far less effective against surface ships, but they fought hard with what they had.

Rusty got a fix on the *Yamato* and corrected their course. Racing in from the flank, the *Sandtiger* still had the element of surprise. They could do this.

Still…

"Conn, Bridge. Have the yeoman report to me on the bridge."

The sailor popped from the hatch and handed him, Rusty, and the quartermaster flak jackets. "You wanted me, Captain?"

"Yeo, I want you to get all the ship's documents ready to deep six."

"Aye, aye, Captain."

"And do it quietly."

If there was a probability of capture, it was his duty to destroy any important documents that would prove useful to the Japanese.

"Do you think this might be a one-way trip?" Rusty said after the yeoman disappeared down the main hatch.

His friend was no doubt thinking about his wife and son.

Charlie put on the flak jacket over his Mae West. "We're going to shoot our entire wad at the *Yamato*. Then we're going to dive. The odds aren't as bad as they look."

"No choice anyway, is there?"

Charlie knew, if Rusty were in command, he wouldn't walk away either. He might survive the war only to be unable to live with himself. He wouldn't ask Charlie to walk away now.

"No choice," Charlie agreed.

"Dumb idea, both of us being on the same

boat. Your letter to Evie is in my pocket. I've been carrying it around these last two patrols."

"We wrote them when we were together on the 55. And we both made it home. Remember, I'm your good luck charm."

"Yeah," said Rusty, no doubt now wondering if he'd been right about that. "You know, just in case, I should say..." The man searched for the right words.

"Save it for after the fight. We're going to get out of this." He called down to Morrison, "Choose your own targets. And keep it hot!"

Morrison grinned. "Aye, aye, Captain."

The din of the battle vibrated in his chest. The ships grew larger with each passing minute. Off the port bow, enemy tin cans fired broadsides into a crippled American DD. The destroyer flew apart under the blows, but kept firing.

Beyond, a squadron of Avengers howled through a wall of flak. One disintegrated and flamed into the sea. A heavy cruiser rocked as bombs exploded on its deck. Another shuddered as a torpedo blast geysered above its hull.

Charlie pointed. "Rusty, conn us into that squall there."

"Aye, aye."

"Morrison! Stand by on the gun! Target to port! Fire at will!"

"Aye, aye!"

The *Sandtiger* knifed into the squall. Rain pounded the deck. In the murk, the bright flashes of cannon fire.

A Japanese light cruiser materialized in the gloom. Rusty swore and shouted orders to the helmsman to avoid collision. They were so close Charlie clearly saw Japanese sailors run across the decks, pointing. One raised a rifle and fired. The round pinged off the conning tower, too close for comfort.

Morrison opened fire at close range, scoring hits as the submarine barreled past. The gunnery officer danced and whooped as the five-inch gun pounded out shells that smashed into the cruiser in clouds of debris. The Bofors and Oerlikon guns banged away, sweeping the main deck.

The surprised cruiser poured on speed and veered off. The *Sandtiger* passed the American destroyer the IJN ship had been fighting. It was the *Johnston*, hammered beyond recognition and ablaze, its mast crumpled over the superstructure.

The bloodied crew raised their fists and cheered as the *Sandtiger* cruised past, Old Glory waving from her shears. Charlie saluted them, struck by the incredible bravery of these men who knew they weren't going home but refused to give up.

Robert E. Lee's quote again. To be a good soldier, you must love the army. He might have added, enough to die for it.

Then the squall swallowed them, and nothing was visible astern except for another round of gun flashes as the Japanese closed in. The boat trembled at the deep concussions of the artillery around them.

The *Sandtiger* emerged from the squall in time to see another American destroyer punching a battleship seven times its size. They disappeared together in rain and mist. Beyond, a wave of planes dropped from the gray clouds to deliver their payloads onto the Japanese ships.

Three heavy cruisers were on fire, one limping away from the battle, the other two listing and blasting their horns as they sank. The destroyers' maniacal defense, coupled with the smokescreens, scattered rainsqualls, and constant harassment from the air, were confounding the Japanese. Their formation had broken up, resulting in piece-meal action.

But it wasn't enough to stop them. The north-ernmost escort carriers were already under attack, hitting back with their single five-inch guns. Three destroyer escorts launched torpedoes at a cruiser before veering off toward the carriers, fighting their bitter rearguard action.

The *Yamato* continued to close in, its mighty guns roaring. Charlie gasped at a massive explosion to the south, though he couldn't see what got hit. His ears popped as the pressure wave rolled over the boat.

Morrison fired his gun a second before the lookouts began calling out contacts.

Japanese destroyers streamed toward the *Sandtiger* from all directions, intent on protecting the *Yamato*.

The submarine had been spotted, the element of surprise gone.

Now it was a race to shoot her torpedoes before the enemy destroyers surrounded her and rained hell.

CHAPTER THIRTY-TWO

DANCE WITH DEATH

Charlie affixed his binoculars to the target-bearing transmitter mounted on the bridge. "This will be a bow shot. Forward Torpedo, make ready the tubes. Order is one, two, three, four, five, six. Set depth at fourteen feet, high speed."

The *Sandtiger* trembled as the outer doors opened and seawater flooded the tubes.

He repeated the command for the aft torpedo tubes, setting the depth at two feet. He'd use them against the enemy destroyers.

"Hook, I want you on the aft TBT," Charlie told the quartermaster.

"Aye, Captain."

"At what range do you want to shoot?" Rusty said.

"We need to get close enough the *Yamato* can't evade our fish. If we miss, this is all for nothing. Maybe 1,500 yards, but I'll take what I can—"

The sea erupted as a shell struck the water

close aboard. The *Sandtiger* jumped at the shock. Shrapnel pinged off the hull.

A Japanese destroyer had barreled in off the starboard beam and fired. Another hill of water rose from the sea off the port quarter, spraying across the deck.

Charlie wheeled. Four destroyers were circling him like sharks, darting in to fire their bow gun before wheeling away to shoot again with their stern gun. Morrison banged away at them with the deck gun. Rusty shouted a constant stream of orders to fishtail the boat and keep her stern aimed at the nearest enemy, a delicate dance in which one false step could result in their destruction.

The destroyers could take multiple solid hits. The *Sandtiger*, with her neutral buoyancy, likely only one. Both ship types had speed on their side, but the submarine had the advantage of being compact and low profile. As long as she kept moving, she was hard to hit, especially when she was firing back.

Which went both ways. He and Hooker fired both of the boat's remaining stern torpedoes, but the nimble destroyers evaded them easily. That was okay. It bought him the breathing room he needed to make his run at the *Yamato*.

After that, he shot his bubblers from their ports on the beam. Thinking they were torpedoes, the destroyers scattered again, offering him a clear path to his target.

Charlie returned his attention to the TBT. The *Sandtiger* was closing in on the giant battleship. She was performing beautifully. After so many failures during the patrol, the battered sea wolf was now hunting at her best efficiency.

Another shell struck the water close aboard, hurling a wall of water across the deck.

Then a destroyer sliced across his path, blocking his view.

"Keep her so," Charlie snarled. "Steady on this course."

More splashes soared around the boat, raining back down. The enemy destroyer grew larger by the second. A shell ripped the air overhead.

Rusty gripped the coaming. "You aren't going to ram him, are you?"

"All guns aimed to port!" Charlie said. "Right full rudder!"

The boat turned hard to starboard, bringing the *Sandtiger* parallel with the enemy destroyer under a smoke-blackened sky. Only a hundred yards separated the two ships. Blue-uniformed Japanese sailors scrambled on the decks, gaping and screaming. The Americans roared back.

They couldn't miss.

"Commence firing!" Charlie cried.

"Fire!" Morrison bellowed.

The *Sandtiger* opened up with every gun she had, raking the destroyer's flank from bow to stern with devastating shellfire. Bodies and clouds of debris flew into the water.

Smoking, the destroyer drifted away without steering.

"Left full rudder! Well done! Rusty, conn us back to a ninety track. Target is still the *Yamato*."

Planes howled overhead. Charlie glanced up in time to see a Japanese Zero dive from the clouds and shriek toward the *Sandtiger*.

"Zeke-type plane, near! Shoot it down!"

The Bofors and Oerlikon guns cranked skyward and poured a stream of shells into the sky. The Zero shied at the tracers but didn't veer off. Nor did it fire.

It carried a bomb.

The plane wobbled under the withering AA fire, trailing smoke.

Something about its angle was wrong.

"He's coming right at us," Charlie said.

Rusty shrank from the coaming. "Christ, he's— he's going to ram!"

They ducked as the plane screeched over-head. Its wing disintegrated as it sliced off the shears. The impact rocked the men to the deck. Shards of metal sprayed the bridge like shrapnel as the plane cartwheeled into the sea with a terrific splash. The bomb exploded, launching a massive spray.

Shaking, Charlie rose to his feet on the wobbling deck. The shears were just gnarled stumps. The lookouts who'd been perched on them were gone. The two petty officers who'd been standing behind him lay groaning on the deck.

"Men overboard," he gasped, knowing they couldn't have survived the impact. "Casualties! We need Doc up here on the double."

Morrison was still firing, so the gun crew was all right.

"Hook's dead," Rusty said.

The man lay on the deck, his head obscenely missing. Blood splattered the deck and coaming.

He looked up. They were just 3,000 yards from the *Yamato*. The three remaining enemy destroyers were making a desperate dash to cut him off.

He wasn't going to let the ship get away.

"We've almost got him!"

The *Sandtiger* raced the destroyers toward the *Yamato*. The range closed.

This was it.

At last, David was ready to do battle with Goliath.

CHAPTER THIRTY-THREE

FIRE ALL TORPEDOES!

The *Yamato* loomed in Charlie's binocular view. Charlie centered the TBT's crosshairs under the massive smokestack belching black smoke.

"Stand by, Forward! Helm, all ahead one-third!"

The battleship's eighteen-inch gun turrets swiveled in his direction. David had Goliath's full attention.

One hit by those massive shells would obliterate the *Sandtiger* and send her wreck plummeting to the bottom.

Too late, he thought. I've got you.

He pressed the transmit button, sending the target bearing down to the TDC. "Constant bearing, mark! Range, 1,700 yards!"

As close as he'd be able to get and still get his shots off.

"Set!" Percy called back.

"Fire all torpedoes!"

Below, Percy punched the firing plunger. "Firing one!" The boat shuddered as she hurled her first torpedo into the water. "One's away!"

Charlie kept the TBT zeroed on the *Yamato*'s hull.

"Firing two!"

The *Sandtiger* bucked as her second fish fled the tube and streaked toward its target.

"Firing three! Firing four!"

One by one, the remaining fish shot into the water, emptying the tubes.

"Firing six! Six is away!"

"Secure the tubes," Charlie ordered. "All ahead flank! Rig to dive!"

The last fish went erratic almost as soon as it launched from the tube. The Mark 18. It broached and banged across the swells, veering off course from the bow to starboard. In silent rage, Charlie watched it go.

He still had five shots reaching for the target, all of them running hot, straight, and normal. He could still do this. What he couldn't do was worry about it. Extricating the boat from this hornet's nest demanded every ounce of his ability and energy. He wanted to dive, but the destroyers were within ramming range. He'd have to fight them off until he gained enough room to pull the plug.

He scanned the scene and knew what he had to do. He'd conn the boat between the *Yamato* and the *Musashi*, and dive there. The *Yamato* was trying to pivot away from the torpedoes, which would add to the confusion. The Japanese admiral's flagship was leaving the line.

Go ahead and turn, he gloated. I've got you.

About to give the command to steer the boat, he froze.

The Mark 18 had arced in seconds, guided by its jammed vertical rudder. He traced its future path, ignoring the heavy shells that splashed around him.

"Right full rudder!" he screamed. "Hard-a-starboard!"

A circular run.

"Jesus Christ," Rusty said.

Their only hope was to swing out of the erratic torpedo's way. Luckily, the Mark 18 was slower than the Mark 14, giving them a fighting chance.

The crew responded in an instant, but fishtailing a submarine took longer than the few seconds he had.

The four big engines roared. Smoke gushed from the exhaust vents. The submarine fought against its momentum, swinging to the right.

Charlie gripped the bridge coaming. "It's going to be close."

"Real close," Rusty gasped.

Sometimes, you get lucky, Charlie prayed.

The torpedo leaped and splashed through the water.

"Um," he said.

She wasn't going to make it.

"Rig for collision!"

Reynolds, the S-55's exec, once told him your life flashes before your eyes when you face the reaper.

That's not what happened to Charlie.

Instead, he thought of all the lives he might have led if he hadn't come here to die in the Pacific.

He might have gone home to Evie ready to live an ordinary life. They'd have bought a house, raised a family, and grown old and contented together. He'd have been a man shaped by war, but he'd have buried the war somewhere deep and let it go.

He might have stayed in Hawaii and waited for Jane. They'd have drank and caroused on the beach until their mutual comfort healed their scars. Together, after finding themselves in war, they'd have found themselves again in peace.

So many possibilities, so many lives.

He now wished he'd heard what Rusty wanted to tell him. Wished he'd told Rusty thank you, and sorry, for everything.

Charlie turned to his friend. "Rusty—"

The torpedo struck the hull near the stern and exploded.

CHAPTER THIRTY-FOUR

THE QUICK AND THE DEAD

The world lurched. The shock slammed Charlie into the coaming. He grabbed and held on to keep from plummeting overboard.

He came to gasping for breath. His binoculars were gone. The world wasn't lurching anymore, but something wasn't right. It was tilting.

And something else. The *Sandtiger* was slowing, almost dead in the water in a dissipating haze of exhaust.

He shook his head to clear it. "Rusty!"

"Men overboard!" Morrison howled at the deck gun. A moment later, it began firing again, hurling shells at the destroyers.

Rusty sat dazed on the deck, gripping his forehead. "What happened?"

Charlie gazed back at where the Mark 18 had plowed into the starboard quarter and detonated. In an instant, he knew the *Sandtiger* was dying, shrieking as water gushed into her wound. The sea fountained like a geyser above the stern, which was already submerged and shrouded in black smoke. Aft Torpedo was certainly flooded, its crew dead, and possibly Maneuvering and the aft engine compartment.

A few more seconds, and the boat might have evaded her doom. His swing maneuver had resulted in the torpedo striking near the stern rather than amidships. If it had, they'd all be dead right now. At least he'd given the crew a chance.

His head ached as if a hammer had struck it. "Close the conning tower hatch!"

If the boat was going down, they didn't have time to abandon ship. With their neutral buoyancy, submarines dropped like stones when holed. Closing the hatch between the conning tower and the control room sealed the survivors inside but at least gave them a fighting chance to escape the boat if she sank.

And sinking she was, quickly.

Percy yelled up the hatch from the conning tower, "I can't reach Maneuvering! We don't have propulsion or steering!"

"Have you gotten any damage reports?"

"I can't reach anybody!" the man said. "The 7MC is shot. Nothing works! All the lights are dead. We're in the dark down here."

The explosion had hurled half the gun crew

into the sea. Morrison fired another round at a distant target then the gun fell silent. He'd had the sense to close the weapons hatch, but in doing so, he'd cut himself off from his ammunition.

They were dead in the water, helpless, unable to dive, move, fight.

"We're sinking," Rusty moaned. "We're done."

Charlie looked around, his mind scrambling for an option. "We..."

The deck kept tilting as the bow rose. The stern disappeared in the tumultuous foam. Beyond, the *Yamato* sailed on in indifference, preoccupied with its turn to dodge the torpedoes. Then Charlie spotted an approaching destroyer, the V of its bow slicing the water with a pronounced wake as it raced in to ram.

"God help us all," he said.

The *Sandtiger* crackled and groaned. She had only moments before the weight in her stern dragged her to the seafloor.

Five thousand fathoms down.

He had to try to get the men out.

"Abandon ship," he said.

He hauled out the soundman, who had a broken arm, followed by Percy and the helmsman.

"Swim," he told each man as he emerged trembling from the hatch. "If you swim hard, you might make it to shore."

Nixon gaped up at him in terror.

"Hurry!"

The boat fell from under him.

"Charlie!" Rusty cried behind him. "The sea—"

The water surged over them and slammed Nixon back down the ladder into his shipmates. Charlie fought against the flood until it dragged him away from the hatch and out into the swirling black of the Pacific. He thrashed, fighting to pull off his flak jacket, sinking like a rock into the darkness.

Then he was drowning just like in Evie's dream.

He broke the surface gasping for air. He yanked the toggles on his Mae West, which inflated with a cracking sound.

Around him, the other survivors swam away from their sinking ship. Charlie alone stayed behind. Treading water, he watched her die, a part of him dying with her as if that part of him were still aboard.

As the sea swallowed his command, Charlie heard a loud boom as the first of his torpedoes struck the *Yamato*.

HISTORICAL NOTES

The *Proteus* would not have worked on the *Sandtiger* or the *Harder*. This submarine tender supported the Twentieth Submarine Squadron, and these submarines were in the Fourth. The *Proteus* mostly worked at Midway and Guam. I included the ship in the story so Charlie could meet a crewman named Bernard Schwartz, a young sailor who would go on to become the famous actor Tony Curtis.

On a *Gato*-class submarine like the *Sandtiger*, the inclinometer, which measured list, was located in the control room, not the conning tower. For dramatic effect, I placed it there so Charlie could see firsthand how far his boat was listing during the typhoon. Note otherwise that, while submarines operated in accordance with strict procedures and protocols, I took quite a bit of license for the story. Any errors in the story are mine alone, though some may be intentional.

The circular torpedo run that sinks the *Sandtiger* was a terrifying possibility realized at least thirty times by submarines during the Pacific War. In many cases, the submarine barely escaped destruction. In two cases, it resulted in the torpedo striking and sinking its submarine. These submarines were the *Tullibee* and the *Tang*. The *Tang* was commanded by the submarine ace Dick O'Kane, who'd apprenticed as executive officer of the *Wahoo* under Mush Morton and was considered one of the greatest submarine skippers of the war, if not the greatest.

The Battle of Leyte Gulf (October 23–26, 1944) was the largest naval battle of World War II and, by some standards, the largest in history. Fought in waters off the Philippine islands of Leyte, Samar, and Luzon, it's certainly one of the most fascinating. This battle featured one of the only two battleship-to-battleship fights during the Pacific War, the first use of organized *kamikaze* attacks, and a desperate and heroic fight between American destroyers and Japanese battlewagons.

The Japanese plan (*Sho-Go*, or Victory Operation) entailed using a task force of carriers to decoy Third Fleet north away from Seventh Fleet, which was staging the invasion of Leyte. Admiral Halsey took the bait, which allowed two strike forces to approach Leyte Gulf through the San Bernardino

Strait and the Surigao Strait. The distant battle Charlie and Rusty hear during the predawn hours of October 25 is Third Fleet smashing Admiral Nishimura's southern task force.

Meanwhile, Admiral Kurita's strike force proceeded unhindered through the San Bernardino Strait and approached Seventh Fleet's rear, attacking its "Taffy 3" unit, made up of jeep carriers and destroyers, off Samar. This resulted in one of the most heroic and lopsided battles of the war, as American planes, destroyers, and destroyer escorts fought Japanese battleships and heavy cruisers. The destroyer USS *Johnston* started the desperate defensive action by attacking on its own, hitting a cruiser with torpedoes. This prompted Admiral Sprague, leading Taffy 3, to give the order, "Small boys attack!" Outclassed and outgunned, the rest of the screening ships attacked in a series of suicidal charges, taking fire and disrupting the Japanese formation. The *Hoel* and *Samuel B. Roberts* sank. The *Johnston* fought to the last, finally sinking after a merciless pounding by enemy destroyers.

The ferocity of these ships, coupled with the battle's confusion, suggested to Admiral Kurita that he was facing a part of Third Fleet. He would later claim he received word American carriers were to the north, and he hoped to attack them.

In any case, he broke off contact and issued orders to steam north and regroup.

The battle crippled the Japanese Combined Fleet, opened invasion of the Philippines, and promised Allied dominance of the Pacific for the remainder of the war.

WANT MORE?

If you enjoyed *Hara-Kiri*, continue the adventure by reading the next book in the series, *Over the Hill*. In this final *Crash Dive* book, Charlie is taken prisoner by the Japanese Empire, surviving the horrors of captivity until gaining the opportunity to fight back.

Sign up for Craig's mailing list to stay up to date on new releases. When you sign up, you'll receive a link to Craig's interactive submarine adventure, *Fire One*. This story puts you in command of your own submarine, matching wits with a Japanese skipper...

Learn more about Craig's writing and sign up for his mailing list at www.CraigDiLouie.com. Craig welcomes your correspondence at Read@CraigDiLouie.com.

Turn the page to read the first chapter of *Over the Hill*.

OVER THE HILL

Craig DiLouie

CHAPTER ONE

THE FURY

Captain Charlie Harrison watched the Philippine Sea swallow the *Sandtiger*'s bow. Floating on the surface, his body bobbed on the swells, though his spirit went down with his ship.

A faulty torpedo had sunk his boat.

As the bow disappeared, he hoped the suction of his sinking command might drag him to the bottom with her. There was only a gentle tug, like a farewell, followed by a swirl of bubbles boiling to the surface and a blooming oil slick.

Suspended in the current, Charlie had become a fly on a vast tapestry of violence still playing out all around him. Steel leviathans filled his view, blasting their giant guns. Tremendous splashes soared past their gunwales. Planes roared through the smoky sky, dodging tracers and shedding bombs that fireballed across decks.

The destroyer that had been intent on ramming the *Sandtiger* raced toward him. In the distance, a heavy cruiser, flying the Rising Sun, exhaled an angry burst of steam as it sank into the foam. Beyond, the *Yamato* lurched on, blasting its whistle as it continued to veer out of formation.

Hit twice by torpedoes, the battleship had a slight list but still afloat. Charlie had failed to sink the giant, but he'd put it out of action for now.

He wheeled in the water toward his own side of the conflict and saw the *USS Johnston* dying.

Hardly recognizable as a warship now, the destroyer was a burning husk racked by internal explosions. Japanese destroyers paced in a semicircle around it, enfilading it with their five-inch guns. The heroic DD rolled until it capsized and began to sink. An enemy tin can moved in to deliver the *coup de grace*.

After a heroic stand, the American destroyers had been wiped out, and despite the *Sandtiger*'s Hail Mary attack against the Japanese flagship, there was nothing to stop the Japanese juggernaut now.

He spun again, treading water, as the enemy destroyer loomed overhead, its gray steel V stirring up a pronounced bow wake. From the forecastle, Japanese sailors wearing dark blue winter uniforms gazed at him.

One by one, they raised bolt-action rifles and aimed.

It's okay, he told himself.

He didn't sink his boat. He didn't kill most of his sixty-man crew. A jammed rudder on a faulty torpedo did.

Go ahead. Do it.

It didn't change the fact he was the one who'd pulled the trigger.

Spike, Braddock, and rest of the *Sandtiger*'s able crew were now either dead or trapped in a metal coffin bound for the bottom of the Philippine Sea. Rusty, Morrison, and the rest of the men who'd escaped were missing, out of sight.

Take your best shot.

Charlie wasn't sure what came after this, but it offered a sure release from hell.

They didn't shoot. The destroyer lowered a whaleboat from the side.

He ignored it, entranced by the sky. A drifting pall of black smoke dimmed the rising sun to a hazy disc.

Then hands grabbed him and hauled him from the sea. Dumped him like a wet rag on the boat's deck.

Japanese sailors stared down at him with contempt.

He was now a prisoner of the Empire.

ABOUT THE AUTHOR

Craig DiLouie is an author of popular thriller, apocalyptic/horror, and sci-fi/fantasy fiction.

In hundreds of reviews, Craig's novels have been praised for their strong characters, action, and gritty realism. Each book promises an exciting experience with people you'll care about in a world that feels real.

These works have been nominated for major literary awards such as the Bram Stoker Award and Audie Award, translated into multiple languages, and optioned for film. He is a member of the Horror Writers Association, International Thriller Writers, and Imaginative Fiction Writers Association.

Learn more at CraigDiLouie.com.

Printed in Great Britain
by Amazon

82108612R00161